nothing is better than god.

c.r.heist

FACT:

All characters and events in this book – even those based on real historical people – even those based on real mythological figures created by real historical people – are entirely fictional.

1

It would seem that this whole thing is as we conceive of it. As if the world actually is what we describe it to be. That it really exists in the way we think it does (*at any one time*). I originally came to tell them that it did not. But I failed. When I was last there I told others of this failure and that eventually I would need to come back, but I didn't know when. How could I have? They couldn't even communicate *my failure* to others. The word ashamed does not nearly begin to describe how they must have felt. They could not have possibly even accepted my assertion of failure because of who they thought I was. Who I still think I am. They knew they couldn't tell anyone, or all they had helped me build, and all they still intended to build, would crumble. It should have crumbled.

I know now that a lot of what I did then paved the way for their inability to communicate. So they just emphasized that I would come again. They left it at that. They left out how our opposition to a beast would itself become a beast. Their minds were very fragile, and now I understand a lot better why that was the case. I had helped to make them this way, and this made me feel indescribably repentant. I had made their phony reality, and after that momentum had begun even I could not convince them of its incorrectness. I wouldn't make the same mistakes again this time, but I was sure I would make many new ones, and this frightened me. A fear that is many levels beyond what any fear of experience on earth (*in its usual conception*) can deliver.

Every time I traveled like this, the thoughts would be overwhelming in an unexplainably intense manner. I had become used to it, but always there was that profound level of uncertainty that increasingly would never leave you alone. It could not, it was its nature to behave this way, and

4

realizing this was part of the way I became more used to it. So apparently now is the time to go back. I don't have much say in this. At least I'm not sure that I do, or better yet, I'm not sure how I could assert that degree of autonomous control here. My path is not that directly communicated to me as I experience it. All I know now is that I move towards returning. Before I do, I have many places to go, or so I'm told... by something. It doesn't even seem like someone, although at the same time it very much does. But as far as I know, no one is telling me this information. These things are very hard to explain at this time. It can be said that I don't sleep, as far I realize. I don't need sleep here, so it doesn't bother me that much. But I can't help being reminded of a lack of sleep when I look around these great interconnecting paths.

As far as I can remember, the first person I ran into that I could or wanted to talk to, was Friedrich. Don't get me wrong. I loved everyone I saw and found a profound magnificence full of interesting qualities as I passed by all of them. Their appearance alone was enough to make anyone used to the familiar scale of earth stunned to silence. But for some set of reasons I was drawn to Friedrich at this time. He had been standing up against a wall that seemed endless in its stretch. When I got close enough I realized that the wall indeed did stretch endlessly in both directions. He did not seem to notice this, or at least he didn't care. In front of him he did stare at a small tree however, in which what looked like many squirrels were running, forming a pretzel shaped motion throughout the tree. We recognized each other's existence and he said to me, "*You see that? That's a squirrel. How unimportant. And yet look at it.*" I did, and agreed that its motion did look familiar, beyond that of a squirrel. And yet, it was a squirrel. He then transitioned straight to his familiar ways, spouting off, "*I always knew that I'd see you here, and that you, like me, were stuck in the same well. It feels very good to be proven right, particularly in the presence of such an arrogant asshole.*" I told him I agreed. I knew he had not made many of the mistakes that I had, although he had a significant head start in terms of when he appeared relative to when I had my chance.

After I thought this he shifted his tone to a more helpful one, "*I hear you're going back into the mix, and since I'm not busy enough operating on the many scales that I do, I figured I'd assist. Be careful what you say, and how you say it. Assume that anyone you talk to will either misunderstand what you say or intentionally twist your statements. And remember that this is not necessarily an undesirable thing. But remember that it is a definite thing. You yourself have been repeatedly mischaracterized. You must know this well. The few accounts of your life are sequenced one after the other recounting differing stories. There are similarities, but there are many differences as well. Some are foundation-shattering contradictions. As you know, I've denied your status on more than one occasion.*"

I found it strange and yet at the same time oddly comforting that he should still question my status, within this place, knowing what we both know now just by being here. Although even in this place, you always know there's an increasingly large amount that you still don't know.

"*You cannot stop people from misrepresenting you after or during your life. You cannot even stop people from misunderstanding what you said or wrote. There will always be benefits to changing your original intentions, misstating your ideas, and making you appear to be something very different from what you really were. You must be very familiar with this. It has probably happened to you more than almost anyone else. I wonder if it angers you. For me, I understand it. I knew they would do it. I knew they would make me look like whatever they wanted to, and that there was no way that I could stop it. I even wrote about this very*

inevitability, to express that even though I was telling who-
ever read me not to do it, I would not be able to prevent it.
Inevitably it would suit someone's interest to use me. I now
understand this even more of course, having seen what you
know I've seen given where you've found me."

I told him I had thought that in my life too (*and*
tried to prevent it via elements of my message) but had
failed to so eloquently communicate it as Friedrich had. I
also clearly had not accepted it as the inevitability that it
was. And would've changed a lot of what I did, had I realized this necessity at the time. And this would've made me
angry had I not also realized my impotence relative to my
time. My failure was understandable. My failure was inevitable. While I could have done better, I could not have done
better enough to significantly alter the path of events on the
high scale I was operating on. What needed to be said at
that time could not have been understood by the people of
that time. This time things are different. What needs to be
said now *can* be understood in the present time. And it can
be said by many people, too many to stop. Back then there
was no basis or foundation for the path of reasoning. And
therefore the necessary line of reasoning would fail, while
later it succeeded in Friedrich's day. How fatalist. Of
course I also knew that there were ways in which I could
have developed the necessary foundation of a path of reason in my day, had I not concentrated on other things that
were not nearly as important as this. Things that actually
were later going to work against my message. Some of
these I even realized at the time, but I was blinded by, I
guess, the overwhelming mysticism of the moment. The
benefits of the lack of a path of reason actually prevented
me from developing one, to receive the vastly more benefits that come from a path of reason. This again made me
very repentant. How could I have known? So little was
known at that time. I thought I was doing well. Friedrich
smiled as I thought.

The smile made me angry. Because I knew the small but certain percentage of his smile that conveyed revenge, and I hate revenge. Not because it was directed against me (*it was, but still...*), but because retaliation was a fundamental emergent extension of a series of reciprocal processes that underwrite the structure of the universe itself. My very opposition to it was itself an example of it. It was going to be there. And the way I tried to deal with it just didn't cut it. My methods were too simple, and too reliant on a non-motivating factor. To see it still around, especially in this place, was very discouraging. Even though I knew why it had to persist. I thought I had solved it. I thought it would be long gone after I was. But it was just beginning. Things were always just beginning. It never stopped. It always got more intense, and harder to deal with. I could never have understood this in my time. And my ignorance caused more damage than I could have ever imagined. I'm in the top ten of all history for manipulations of mind that led to massive amounts of violence. Friedrich knew this. When I thought about this he laughed out loud in my face.

His physical form shook with a petulant vibration as he laughed, extending his material iterations further and with more prominence. Seeing the visual of this made me laugh, and experiencing again the underwritten process of the universe helped me to feel less discouraged. I thanked him for his insights. He immediately replied with a well planned and beautifully executed, *"go fuck yourself."* Where we were, there was much more time to work with. I told him I didn't need any more help right now.

2

There is too much repetition in existence for anyone to keep track of it all. But at a certain point there is so much repetition that everyone cannot help but notice the patterns (*that were there before, but were too large to discern*) everywhere. I've seen too many paradoxes to stop now. I had left Friedrich on Q Street. When I got over to the Capitol building, I remembered some things. It had been a long time since I'd been to this part of the planet on this scale. The Capitol was grand in its outstretched map of repetitions moving in both directions. I could see it partially burnt in one direction, and partially blown apart not too far off in the other direction. Although the further the repetitions stretched out, the smaller they became, so the burnt Capitol was somewhat off in the distance to the north and about the size that it appears on the American fifty dollar bill.

There were many people around here. Most notable of which were two people playing a game of chess in the strangest of places. They were sitting with a little table right in the middle of one of the two main staircases on the West front side of the Capitol, on one of the few between-step plateaus. I knew them both well, so I was excited to see them again. Benjamin and Burrhus. Two of the best chess players in the history of the world, and with this statement I do not mean to refer only to the commonly known game. No one interrupted the match, although there was a fair amount of traffic. I guess everyone understood. How could they not here? Things actually were well communicated when left unsaid in this place. I looked up atop the stairs of one of the closer, larger future iterations of the Capitol and saw Friedrich leaning against the building laughing while staring at me, smoking a pipe.

Very abruptly Burrhus kicked the table over and proclaimed victory over Benjamin. Benjamin laughed and said, *"There is no victory like a public relations victory! You know I had you beat. And yet you just convinced me that you won! And all you had to do was destroy the game, a deceptive tactic of a five year old."* Burrhus responded, *"Ah but that itself was a ruse unlike one you're familiar with! I pretended to soar-loser you, but in actuality I have distracted you with an overly simple trick, one you could easily figure out, one that would lead you to underestimate me, thinking that I had made mistakes when any mistakes I had made I did on purpose, allowing me to succeed with my more complex tricks. Even my explanation of my trick right now is itself a layer of deception counteracting your ability to assess the reality of the situation!"* We all laughed at this point. Even the people passing by that were seemingly unable to hear started laughing.

    "You know," Benjamin said. *"I know exactly what you're doing. You know that I know what you're doing. You know that you cannot hide anything from me here, especially now. All of your antics are merely comedy relief for spectators from another scale that may or may not be watching us right now for a variety of purposes. I do appreciate the network of deceit you laid out before me, quite visibly if I might criticize, for its complexity. But it cannot succeed in the manner you're used to succeeding in on this scale. And you know that too."* *"I do not know that!"* Burrhus reacted immediately. *"If I know anything, even in this place, it is because I have been conditioned to know it, by something that is benefiting from this conditioning in some way. So I choose to behave as if I do not know it. Because all of my knowledge is tainted with these many other things' purposes."* Burrhus turned to me, *"This is at least partly your fault... you were supposed to arrange things on a scale below us a long time ago that would've already helped to transform this scale back to where it should be. My antics, as Benjamin calls them, would return to their usual state of superiority in this arena had you done this. I*

do not need to be told how I was wrong anymore. I can see it everywhere. But apparently, you still do. You were wrong. You were a causal agent in something very important, and you ducked that position of deterministic responsibility. How could you? I'm not asking how could you in the usual sense, as to the role of your intent. I'm asking how in the hell did it happen in time itself? How were temporal conditions allowed to give you the opportunity to miss your opportunity? To rest that massive amount of dynamical weight on your life is ludicrous. It doesn't seem like it would be set up that way. This very event sequence right now does not seem like it is statistically feasible to occur. We are being undone. So get back there, and fix what you broke! Damn, it did it again... forget everything I just said! I don't want to help this deceiver."

3

"*I am the way of productivity that will make you fail!*" pronounced Burrhus laughing aloud while screaming towards the sky. Benjamin had sat patiently through his entire tirade, smiling subtly. He had more than enough time to prepare a response now, because of the changes his match partner was yelling about. They always had an increased amount of time here, but because of a certain situation it had increased even more so. In fact, the very reason such great minds had descended to their current scale, just one time scale above where earth as people know it sat, was because of this unresolved situation. Under 'normal' circumstances, if you can even call it that, these minds would be a few scales larger in complexity from here, dealing with more profoundly important measures that expand and uphold the integrity of the universe. But here they were, hanging out in very unusual circumstances for all of them. Even though they were all very familiar with this place, they were used to being beyond this place most of the time, and being 'stuck' here upset some of the more ornery mental signals. To be honest though most of them didn't seem to care, including Benjamin.

"*Every once in a while you must recalibrate.*" Benjamin said. "*Don't underestimate what you know isn't true. The freedom to reorganize is paramount. I still think Burrhus has to be told how he was wrong. That will help you when you go back.*" Burrhus sat pouting on a step as Benjamin spoke. "*As you'll all remember, autonomy is not as simple as it had been conceived of for so long. We are not being undone. We are doing what has always been done. We are adapting to an increasingly complex environment. We are seeing liberty assert itself in existence. We are experiencing change as we always have, unpredictably. Although our pouting friend likes to believe otherwise, in-*

determinism plays just as significant a role as determinism does in this universe. And indeterminism is freedom. It is one half of the trial and error process, the trying and the errors part. The learning part... The other half of course is the part that the trial and error occurs in. This is the environment of events that were already underway on different deterministic paths, those events that were waiting to be changed. Even the fact that indeterminism is a natural feedback response to deterministic forces does not negate its freedom. Every time a free action is realized as being caused largely by deterministic forces, this realization does not remove its freedom. It gives us the freedom to reorganize according to that new information about deterministic forces we were unfamiliar with before. Freedom & determinism persist endlessly in an infinite feedback bounce. The great physicist/philosopher Fuckus described it like infinitely extending 'accelerated event sequences' in shapes similar to double helixes of DNA, in 2018. When a conscious entity is able to perceive an unwanted or wanted determinism, it can reorganize itself to avoid or move towards it. The skill in increasing freedom is the expansion of our realizations of the increasingly complex deterministic framework we operate within. When we begin we are largely determined, but we can reorganize that determinism. And even though we are conditioned (determined) to reorganize our deterministic maps, we are free to reorganize this conditioning, even though that too was determined given that level of understood information. And so on forever. Each leap in reorganization in this sense gets increasingly more difficult, like the limits experienced folding a sheet of paper in half indefinitely. Which, by the way, can be done indefinitely. You just need increasingly more math and technology to continue doing it."

"*Yeah, well 2018 may have been just a little too late to deal with and/or reverse some very critical institutional processes on earth.*" Burrhus retorted. "*It's never too late.*"

replied Benjamin. Suddenly I noticed what would normally be described as a commotion near the edge of the steps of the building. For some reason the Capitol building, on this scale, sat on the edge of a great chasm that spilled down just off the west side at least about 100 feet. I hadn't remembered this before, but it was there now. Or at least, this had been abruptly made noticeable to me at this time, and for the first time. Someone was very drunkenly flopping around the edge of this pit, too close to the edge, his event path shifting in multiple directions at once but for not too long of distances. He was emitting almost a visual thought screen there were so many voices of him at once, *"I told people exactly how to do it. And even though so many people have read about and understand these tactics down to a science, nobody prevents them from being used. Even in so-called democracies. Everyone is still afraid. It never stops working. There are so many layers of phony superiority contributing to the ease of manipulation. People still don't understand the simple relationships that exist between them in groups. They don't know how easy it is to divide them, and just as easy to make them band together. All motion attracts or repels."* He looked like a spider made up of 6 human 'spider legs', each leg trying to go in a different direction. If there was a way to visually represent an ultimate confusion, this man's motion fit the bill. As he approached the edge of this cliff his form moved back towards that of one man.

"Who is that man thrashing about near the edge yelling?" I asked Burrhus. *"Oh... that's Niccolo. Don't mind him. He's just better at doing what I was just trying to do."* As he said this he moved closer to him. *"He realized when he first came here that each time he dies from here he accelerates to a greater extent the depth of complexity he moves into. So he keeps killing himself in different ways to get more power and experience more control over this place and the universe in its wider sense. Even though he*

14

knows that along with every jump in complexity there exists a corresponding jump in responsibility, locking his power into activities he must constantly accomplish. He knows that this draw toward power is a temporal trick that draws toward enslavement to a set of new and more complex tasks. He fills his experience past capacity as fast as he can, with the obvious result of ending his experience every time he gets back here. He has locked himself into this increasingly more repetitive pattern. Usually he succeeds in moving forward, but he keeps popping back here somewhere every time now. When you rectify things his ascent will continue. All of our trajectories will improve. But for the time being he's locked himself into this unnecessary rut due to his immense momentum. And who are we to step in his way?" As he said this he put his foot out in such a perfectly timed motion that it looked as if it had been rehearsed a hundred times before. His outstretched foot caught Niccolo's leg as he thrashed by, tripping him over the edge he was so dangerously close to. The drop was very far indeed, and Niccolo cheered the whole way down, his body's form tweaking with dissipation (*I think because of anticipation*) as he approached what he hoped would be another (*even more complex*) scale transition.

4

This sort of spectacle would be an important instability in earth's more regular circles, with everyone around very interested, concerned and upset about something so crazy happening in their midst. But here, all acted as if this instability was not that critical of a situation. They in fact treated it as though it was completely acceptable and easily manageable. And no one expressed concern that what Burrhus had visibly done was wrong or of any value at all (*negative or positive*) really. Even Benjamin. I guess Niccolo knew what he was doing. And since I couldn't get caught up in what was going on here anymore, I walked away thinking about other things before Niccolo reappeared, again. I didn't fully understand everything I was experiencing, and I wasn't sure what pieces of information, if any, I would need later. I had to get back to earth in the present. I had to stay focused.

Space and time operated in a much more flexible manner here, and their interconnectedness was quite visible. We were on a scale somewhat but not nearly completely beyond time. So you could see time as long chains of repetitions in space (*because, it is a part of space, and vice versa*). You could see more of the waves of iterations for every thing and every event that thing underwent. So to describe how it looked, while difficult, was not total nonsense. Long distances were also easily stepped into without the usual delay that distance tends to create when you're on the cusp of the ever-expanding present. And it was much more difficult to tell whether anything was something unique, or merely a repetition of something else. The lines of individuality of object were blurred. Yet there was no question that the individual items within space-time were still unique entities. Like I said, it was very difficult to describe. Things were quite clearly nonlinear. An object could hold a simultaneous state of a percentage of a material iteration of something else *and* a percentage of originality emerging from mere repetition. In fact the line where originality began and repetition stopped was entirely relative to scale and level of detail.

All lines blurred, and this made me think of how dependent on lines we still are in the present. The fact that we use a straight line to describe so much of our experience is evidence of the insufficient nature of our descriptions. Thinking this drew me to some of my earlier representations of reality. I could not help but remember the flaws of my message as I had delivered it my first time around. The simplicity of it devastated me. The absolute property of my ranting and the authoritative, and sometimes threatening ways in which I delivered the ideas that were supposedly true made me again fall to my knees begging forgiveness, even though I had known now for some time that there was no point in doing this. When one begs for forgiveness to no person, they are deferring the responsibility of their actions, avoiding the accountability to the real people they may have harmed. You can convince yourself that you've really paid your debt, just by apologizing to someone that isn't there. The people that are there (*the people you avoided by begging forgiveness only from a non-existent person*) are left damaged and any injustice is left unresolved.

This reminded me of one of my most prominent philosophies that billions of people later adopted. God the damage I must've done with that. I think the main reason I'm the one that has to go back is that I'm the one that messed it up the most. Even though, like I've said, my ignorance was understandable (*and common*) at that time in history. This particular pillar of my supposedly absolutely true thoughts became known as '*the golden rule*': *Do unto others as you would have them do unto you.* It's not like I really even wrote the damned thing. I swiped it from other historical prophets I liked from before my time. I knew it played well with crowds and intellectuals alike, so I reworded it and called it my own thought. Again, I'd say it was a combination of repetition and originality, admittedly though more toward the 'copying someone else' side of that coin.

But it was incomplete. Horribly so... With consequences even the manipulative me at the time couldn't have possibly understood. Even though I'd somewhat ripped it off, the *do unto others as you would have them do unto you* thing hadn't really caught on in societies as a principle yet. The going philosophy at the time in most places was still the Hammurabic code. *An eye for an eye.* That most initial of all proclamations of justice... I guess it was really just the first time the thought of absolute and direct reciprocity had formally been applied to a legal system within one of the earliest human societies. Although the code of Hammurabi was later abandoned for more nonlinear & complex rectifications of grievances rather than the exact same action that was the crime being used as *the* punishment administered in response, my golden rule had not been able to replace it. It, just as *an eye for an eye*, was too simple for the law. But it had a different, more profoundly important use. It made people more submissive to exploitation, whether on a small or large scale. Turning the other cheek turned out to be the best tool powerful people had in their arsenal to insure that there was no response to their continued oppression. This is one of the reasons I think the Roman Empire so quickly adopted my philosophies after executing me.

What more could a power hungry control-freak empire ask, from its populations of socially imposed lower classes, than a response of acting toward the empire as they would like the empire to behave. Not in direct response to how the empire is behaving, which would undoubtedly produce opposition. But by turning the other cheek... the fact that this sort of religious philosophy worked in this respect probably astonished the elite classes that were exploiting the majority of their peoples. Manipulating minds turned out to be way more powerful than controlling people with more direct methods of suppressing opposition. In a funny way, even though I never came close to pursuing, let alone attaining any such official position, I think ideologically I was the most powerful emperor Rome ever had. Had they not been so quick to execute me, I might have ended up being the emperor, and the first pope, instead of Peter. It's so sad how power works. Even when you don't mean to, you can aid that which you're really in opposition to. This inevitably happens because events are nonlinear. There is not as much 'total opposition' as people think in entities that are dynamically opposed to each other. Nothing is absolute. I wasn't sure if I was trying to convince myself of all these things, or if I was somehow figuring them out, or if my thoughts were just setting up elements of my future. Even though there are probably many reasons for thoughts to be produced, I couldn't stop them from being released at this time.

In a dynamical sense the code of Hammurabi could be seen as a motion of direct reciprocal response to actions taken against an entity, I thought. You get hit ... you hit back. My golden rule can be seen as a motion of no reciprocal response to actions taken against an entity. You get hit.... you *do not* hit back. Both of these should be obviously insufficient. The code of Hammurabi lasted for over a thousand years and then was abandoned. Its tit-for-tat method didn't work in a legal system, but societies kept it around for a variety of other purposes. But apparently human beings so far have thought my rule was quite sufficient for two thousand years. As I've already said, this is not because it worked (*for what it is said to work for*) but because it was useful to powerful people in maintaining systems of control. The future does eventually spell out other alternatives. Scientists in the area of nonlinear dynamics have already (*in the present*) developed certain alternatives. They were able to create computer models of many simulated entities interacting with specified reciprocation rules to study the possibilities of better solutions. And they found some. They mostly involved multi-event reciprocation patterns. One example: If you got hit, you did not hit back the first time, but if that same entity hits you again you hit back that second time. This was to account for the possibility (*inevitability*) that accidental hits would occur between entities. This is still relatively simple and you can see how such models have developed toward greater complexity from here, accounting for all sorts of situational commonalities at the same time.

The interesting question people then usually ask is, "Why have I not heard of these alternatives?" And the more compelling question, "Why then do powerful institutions on earth that know these more complex solutions exist, continue to operate in the very simplest reciprocal patterns?" The answer to both of these questions is what I said before. Because doing so is useful to powerful people in maintaining systems of control. All ruling structures make people use over-simplistic methods of interaction (*by not communicating the better ways*) because there are great benefits to receive that people in general are not at all aware of. I could hear Friedrich laughing, even though he was not around. And I was no longer anywhere near what would look like Washington D.C. on earth anymore.

5

Experiencing perception here was kinda like looking at time-lapse photography, except instead of blurs of things in motion there were always many solid representations of the same thing connected via blurs, reflecting a certain span of time, each repetition getting smaller on each side as they faded in the different directions of before and after the current present. On earth in the present, as the two thousand years went by, people that followed my teachings became more and more oppressive, of themselves and each other. My teachings twisted into justifications for every further act of violence, every further act of autocracy... I was sickened by watching it... The authorities representing me became more and more powerful... every church, every monarchy, almost every empire... they all propped themselves up on me.

Even back in the day, when I was alive for the first time, I hated the fact that people *followed* me. But at those times, like things exist still, in order to build organizations you needed followers. You needed people who would joyfully do what no independent person would accept doing. You needed the multi-level marketing effect of friend-to-friend and family member-to-family member sales indoctrination. If people didn't follow the organization in a sociopathic manner, spreading it furiously as far as they could, you would be out-competed by rival organizations. Those organizations that were willing to create the most vehement followers of their *purpose* scored the highest gains. Their institutions grew larger faster and they swallowed the others. Fanatics were what people wanted. They built more effective organizations. As the social structures these networks of organizations existed within became more and more autocratic, the value of fanatics had become increasingly clear. Why would you waste time arguing over any details when an absolutely efficient order could be produced with mere total submission to a hierarchy. That's what they must have thought, anyway.

It was though I was walking through the desert again. It even looked like a desert to me, although I'm not sure what it was. But I'll describe it anyways. Vast lands of emptiness as far as could be seen, and I could even see beyond the usual obstacle of the curvature of the earth. It was still empty beyond the curve, except for pyramid shaped rock formations every once in a while with pieces chunked out of them caused by natural disasters and the weather effects of a thousand years, or through the effects of political structures operating in the vicinity for thousands of years. Strangely, here, it was hard to tell the difference. They seemed like very similar forces. Even in vast emptiness there was repetition of structure. In fact, there was *more* frequency of repetition in structure, within spaces of vast emptiness. There was more order. I started to notice how in nature, something with repetitive organization that moves more toward an absolute order, was empty.

I don't know why I even try to describe this place at all. It's just my skewed perception of it. For all I know I could be seeing things. And my descriptions would most likely only be used against you in later years anyway. That's what always happens. As if the way I was able to describe where I've been and what I think is perfect. Like everything I say is true. (As if it's right at all.) How could that be, even for a god? It takes time to describe places and things, and there are always more details that could be mentioned. So is something true when it's incomplete? Or does one sit forever listening to god's eternal description of a single event? My followers never saw how this didn't make sense. They knew to obey the authority (*the truth*)… that was all. It could tell them anything, and anything became truth. As long as god's or my name was attached to it… How sad. You could reverse every religious teaching a certain deity professed, and as long as you kept that deity's name attached to the opposite teachings of that deity, most of their followers would still believe you. This demonstrates the depth to which most people even know or experience that which they claim to fanatically believe. Absolutism is more an escape from *any* inquisitive examination, even from that with which you are obsessed. It is the ultimate tool of authoritarians. And any religion that professes truth is vulnerable. Last I looked nearly all religions, even in the twenty-first century, professed that their religion was truth. How very unfortunate for the unfolding sequence of events in the twenty-first century.

Benjamin instantly appeared before me, *"You have just had a very important realization!"* "What, that the world is screwed?" *"No. You have just become cognizant of one of the main reasons we adopted a separation between church and state for America. The main reason that hardly anyone can explain. That government has a long history of usurping religions, taking their followers and switching their beliefs under an absolute authority. That no matter what the religion, if it becomes obsessed with changing and being active in politics, it will become owned by politics. The political order will adopt the religion as its own and change it, and most oftentimes leave an immense trail of blood through history. A church should not want to take sides on issues of the nation it resides in. It should know that by doing so it is rejecting its faith, and handing itself over to authoritarians to mold it for imposing tyranny. We were very careful to prevent such circumstances from happening here. We were victims of the tyranny of the Church of England, a protestant denomination of Christianity that upheld the rule of a tyrannical monarchy. It was a denomination that was created, by the king, for his own superficial reasons of power."*

"And it was not the only one." He continued. *"Just about every denomination of Christianity there is devel-*

oped as a political response to another denomination. Every time it happened it was because a group of people felt as if their beliefs, particularly concerning governance, were different enough to warrant a new church (and the power that easily flows from doing so). They would rally support through opposition to the current church order wherever they lived. And as you well know, this whole protestant movement (meaning protest) spawned originally in response to the tyranny of the Catholic Church. When we structured the American system we thought we could be different. We thought we could prevent this cycle of replacing tyrannical religious orders with new tyrannical religious orders from taking place. We thought that by separating any religious institution from access or connection to government, and allowing the free exercise of any religion's beliefs without any interference from government, that an authoritarian political party using a religion to gain power in a society would never have a chance here in America. We were almost right. We did prevent it for some time. But there were other complexities of society we hadn't enough knowledge of yet."

How he was saying what he was saying made it seem like the information was at the core of his being. *"The truth makes you vulnerable, as you said. Not because it is true. But because it isn't… Any claim of truth is a deception scheme to achieve power over you. If you believe in a religious truth, you have not made a god happy, you have made humans who want to live like gods happy."* Benjamin seemed to know his country well. He also knew a lot about the strange path my original creation had taken since my execution. If I were more honest with myself I would admit to foreseeing some of this when I claimed to be the Messiah all those years ago. And I did it anyway. And now I was going to go back claiming to be the Messiah again. I was *still* an arrogant asshole. Again Friedrich's laughter was unmistakably heard in the distance.

6

People desired a truth. The human mind seeks the stability of knowing that things in their life are exact, complete, and unchangeable. There is a comfort and a function to this ignorance. People liked their descriptions to be simple, clear and concise so that they could use that information to do things. Thinking of the information they received as incomplete or not entirely true interrupted their ability to use the information. And this sort of feeling did not sit well in their minds. *"That is the origin of heaven."* I heard a voice say. He was not talking to me, but somehow what he was saying to other people made sense to what I had just been thinking. I would've thought it was coincidence in the old days, but now I knew a little more about causality (*coincidental correlations do happen all the time, what I mean to imply is that they are also an as of yet undiscovered part of the dynamical structure of causality itself*). I went to listen to what looked like an organically organized speaking engagement (*of some sort*) on the edge of a town that was on the edge of the desert I had been in. Things usually transitioned into existence through edges.

"This is not heaven!" Blake pronounced authoritatively to a crowd of recent arrivals. *"It was only our doors that tricked us into believing it would be so. So now that you are conscious after your life you assume that it is the case. What else could it be? Hah. The next time you feel that question coming on...know that it could be anything! Things can be described in any way you wish, and it is only because you fell under the control of people that chose to direct your descriptions that you did not realize this from whence you came."* The looks on people's faces at times like this are the most priceless. *"We love extremes."* Blake continued. *"We love opposites more than the words we use to fill the empty spaces where we feel opposites must exist!"*

It may seem strange that Blake should assert that there is no heaven, while in this place. Where we were was of course post-life. And yet it was not heaven to him, nor to anyone else I had ever known here. It was not hell, nor purgatory, nor any of the names given to places that supposedly existed after life. Yet *everyone* that died came here. Many of the people hearing this were very uncertain, as this was a new perspective to most of them. They had been riding the present. And that process locks a person into the cluster of events within that scale. Existing continuously on an unfolding path tends to localize the perception of that path. *"Where you are now"*, he asserted, *"is better than heaven! It includes everything that heaven and hell both were thought to encompass, and so much more beyond that."* His recent guests had a tough time believing this. Lucky for him, they didn't need to believe it.

"This is the first lesson," He lectured. *"Belief is based on a latching onto of information, merely a byproduct of a natural nonlinear organizing process."* At this point some of the people wandered off, as was the case most of the time during these impromptu briefing sessions by anybody who cared to conduct them, for people didn't need to do anything they didn't want to here. And that was quite clear to almost all given the enhanced mental scope received upon arrival. I stayed to listen because I liked Blake and I hadn't talked to him in a while. After he finished yelling about things he didn't have to yell about we went to discuss my return to the present. *"I just enjoy it."* He said. *"I know it's not at all necessary, they're just used to hearing things that way. After coming here from that simple place."* I told him I understood and would have to be performing similar antics when I got back to earth. So witnessing it became a helpful reminder. *"You know, I can't believe that something so ridiculous as this is happening. That even though none of it was ever real, we've chosen for you to go back and pretend that it was, to rectify the origi-*

nal damage done. It really is an amazingly absurd thing." "On this point we agree wholeheartedly", I told him, and we laughed at the way even the world beyond the world works.

"Remember," he reminded me, *"that I was one of the first promoters of nonlinearity in my day...even though it wasn't called that back then... and most people were very much against the idea. And that was hundreds of years before where/when you're going back to."* "They study it now", I told him. "I'll let them know about your contribution so you can take credit from here." *"You know I don't want credit."* He thought to himself a moment. *"Then why the hell did I just brag about it? Inertia's a bitch."* We both laughed again. *"Even though it's been so long, I still unknowingly reflect events every once in a while. Things similar to what I had done in the past. And I know why the similarities still repeat to a certain extent, having been here for some time. But it never gets old. This universe is more artistically insane than I ever was."* **"Obviously."** We both said at the same time, laughing.

I remember the thought of hell, on earth, and how useful it was. I remember how people thought they needed to convince other people that hell existed so that they would behave properly. That was the idea's main purpose, Burrhus had told me. But the details of the idea were so seemingly masochistic. It would've been great as a horror story, but back then humans didn't tell each other that stories weren't real. They told them they *were* real. Life must have been so boring initially. Even before larger societies, on a tribal level, there was still an emptiness of ideas. Thought hadn't yet had the chance to create a lot of them. It still hadn't created enough. No matter what the complexity level of the society, living an adventure was much better than hearing an adventure story. This was the first time I had thought that meaning was created.

"*You were supposed to have been to hell.*" Blake reminded me. "*Your partner will help you with that later. Credibility wise 'n all.*" "I don't remember going", I said. "*You didn't go. But it gave credibility to the hell myth by saying that you did go. So that's what people wrote about you. Your partner will fill in all the details to them for you, so as to remove any doubt of who you are upon your return.*" "That's another thing", I said. "I'm still feeling guilty about pretending I was the Messiah the first time I was on earth." "*You should, god damn it!*" He was quick to point out. I told him that I wasn't even really pretending back then, I really thought I was the chosen one. Then I asked him how I would be able to pull it off again knowing flat out that it isn't true? I was sort of lying to Blake here because I did still think that in some ways I was Him. I was at least fulfilling the role of Him, I thought. Blake smiled. "*By knowing that there isn't any chosen one... there is no Messiah. The only reason you're going back is to reverse the lie. And part of reversing the lie is exposing to everyone how you are not Him. So you've got to come to the realization that you're not Him first.*"

Then he smiled even wider. "*The Messiah myth is a part of many religions. Because an individual can easily model her or his behavior off of a character... so simply put, it's a role model story. It gave people an ultimate piousness to work towards, particularly the insane, which usually tended away from piety. It also gave people something to look forward to, or aspire to, in terms of relieving their society's oppression. Many societies have been through hellish experiences, and it is usually out of this that a person or persons cause great change to upend the corrupt system. So of course in the story, you went to hell. But you were such a badass that you came back from it. Remind you of any other hero stories? Do Dionysos, Herakles, Ishtar, Krishna, Orpheus, Persephone, or Quetzalcoatl ring a bell? Any number of movies later made in the twentieth*" *century also fit the bill. It really is ridiculous that anyone with the brain functions that humans have got stuck believing in this pop-culture load of crap. Even way back in your day. Something back then must've made people more afraid than believing in the story of hell ever could have, in order for them to accept that story as real. What that was will be harder to defeat than hell, because I suspect that it still exists, and that you'll have to deal with it when you go back. Once you figure out what it is."*

7

Language throws us into the light and then immediately throws us back into the dark. When we've got something, we think we've got it all. Such is the history of words and concepts. Positions from certain angles of thought blind us to other angles when the iterative momentum builds as we repeat what we already have. We dig ourselves into a hole just by doing what is determined of us. Using what we have. This would commonly be thought of as a sort of paradox if not for the enlightenment of the concept of non-linearity. When the nonlinear is understood, a paradox is only the border of a too simplistic concept. A border to be extended with more complex concepts that uncover a greater understanding of what we thought was already useful. *"Opposites,"* Blake held, *"were understandable attractor basins to fall into. As in, conceptually determined pits that were there to be easily run around in over and over again, the whole time thinking it would be nonsensical to climb out of these pits and dig new more interestingly structured designs to travel in. The first problem is probably that people do not think of language in this way. They think of language as a completed tool to learn and use. Not something that is constantly changing and becoming increasingly complex. They may see language change a little, but not in a significant enough manner to justify pursuing faster change. It's just not something people had the time to delve into, being incredibly busy just trying to use as much of the language they already had available to them, which seemed infinite."*

The number of concepts and words in a language that already exist should by definition be an expanding finite, I thought. They are already being used. They are perpetually written down as created. The incomprehensibility of it all should be a problem of educating people in the near-entirety of their languages, not a problem in any language itself. *"How are uneducated people supposed to realize that?"* Blake added to my thoughts. As if he could read my thoughts. That bothered me at first. Blake smiled at me when I thought this. *"At least you could think about getting past being bothered by it."* "How do you do that?" Of course I asked him that. I suppose he'd know how predictable that question would be. *"Let's just say I'm very skilled at language. Most everyone here is. You're almost there."* "But how does it work?" I couldn't believe how easy it seemed to him. He smiled again. Often people smile when they realize you don't understand something they know well. *"It's really just a complex extension of whatever languages you already know. You'd be surprised how knowing most of the probable thought outcomes of what's said with sound can allow you to anticipate what thoughts are thought to a reasonably accurate degree."* Of course it was complex. It seemed like a difficult skill. *"Nah, it's not that bad. But it takes time. Practice makes _____!"* I'm sure it gets way harder than that one. *"Stop thinking of it as hard. And if you wanna get really good at it, stop thinking that things need to be exact. Estimation is your best friend in this exercise. Thoughts are most often times not words. So you don't need to refine your probability estimates to specific words. And watch how repetition amidst thoughts and the spoken word works in your favor when estimating."*

Damn. I did not expect this. I did not expect something like mind reading to work so logically and rationally. *"It's not that exact, like I said. You're not really mind reading either. You're reading the thought extension probabilities of conversations. But when you get really good at it, you'll be cleverly modifying your conversations to initiate certain conditioned thoughts to see what pathways can exist in different people."* Burrhus would love that, I thought. *"Yes he does. There is no 'would' with that guy. But this shit is distracting us from what we need to focus on. You don't need to worry about developing these skills now. You need to learn more. You need to understand more about what keeps people stuck in less."* "And what's that?" I thought out loud by saying it. *"That... is opposites. When you see the extremes, you see the borders. You see the range within which communication is currently stuck."* I thought about how big the range between opposites is and Blake interrupted my thoughts with words again. *"Not very big at all. When dealing with opposites, to find the big range you need to step outside of the opposing extremes. The range between the opposites is a framed oversimplification. It is very little of what is."*

Thinking is such a pain in the ass. Blake just kept on going even though I'm sure he knew what I was thinking. *"This is not always to say that you extend the extremes. Although this naturally occurs to some extent... A set of opposites is like a pendulum swinging dynamical system. There are two sides to swing to, and there is that which is between the extremes of each side. It is a common pattern in nature, not just in language. A very simple one."* This must be the feeling people get when they give up. It seems too difficult. It takes too much energy to concentrate. And there's so many words. There's not enough time to absorb it all. I'm sliding off the back of the thought wave. I can't pay attention anymore. There is a sense of relief, and a relaxation. It tends to keep me here. It's nicer here. This must be what happens. At the time of mental exhaustion, the high you get keeps you from attempting to use your mind in strenuous ways. Learning too fast conditions you to dislike learning. I'm tired.

"Don't quit on me yet, damn it. You know I've gotta do this!" I know, I know... you're conditioned too. *"Hey, communicating information can be an annoying task, but if you want to do anything it must be done."* I was thinking all of this too but for some reason now it didn't bother me in the same way. It was easier. I had experience on this level.

32

I was more actively a part of it. I was participating in this conversation. Well, I was because Blake could understand me now even though I wasn't talking to him with sound. This place really was intoxicated. *"Yeah it kinda does feel like you're on drugs in the present. But of course I'd say that it's also better than that."* "Of course it would have to be. Right? That's what everyone would expect." When I said this I felt strange. This was the first time I had thought that intelligence was learned.

"Just like language is." Blake said. *"We all start off simple. Intelligence is pretty much the degree to which you master languages."* Back in the day, people considered me a master of language. I astonished them with wisdom. I made them believe in my words with my words. *"We keep getting distracted. Which is something to cherish. It allows you to mix better."* "But you were just rushing! You didn't want to be distracted." *"Yeah I was making a different point then. And at the same time I was setting up this point. So that the point was a clear example... Sorry about all the layering."* He was becoming annoyingly complex, or just annoying. *"You ever hear about exercising your brain? It is a muscle, you know."* I felt as though there was a conflict between us. He seemed aggressive, and I seemed submissive. I taught people to be submissive. I don't feel equal. Why did I teach people to feel less than other people? It's hard for me to remember. But I think back then I really got a kick out of controlling people, whether I knew it then or not. I realize it more than ever now. I wonder what proportion of all people get that same high out of manipulating humans & their events in the present. *"More than ever."* Blake said these words as if he was really pissed. He wasn't upset at me, despite my overly anxious concerns. He was angry that human beings had yet to deal with their incredibly dominating nature.

"It wasn't that humans had a dominating nature to them. All of nature at certain times, and for certain rea-

sons, developed a tendency to be excessively aggressive and to attempt to dominate others. But we know why that happened now. And we know a certain element of domination exists within a certain proportion of the human population. But even though they know the psychology and the biology of it in the present, they allow it to persist. Again the cause is that only a small percentage of all people understand enough. Because the science and information that would enlighten them has not yet reached enough of them."
"Evil." I said out loud. I don't know why I said it then. "*Ignorance.*" Blake said back. "*It's a difficult task to educate millions of people in the hard sciences. But they know how to do that too.*" Science added additional languages to an already insurmountable learning curve. At this point I wondered why educational institutions didn't grow as fast as other more powerful institutions of authority. "*Maybe because their output helps prevent future authorities.*"

"*Look. Free will and fate... Good vs. evil. Right and wrong... Hell, even up and down skew perception away from empirical reality! They're all painfully incomplete. And yet quick decisions are made in the present all the time that rely on only simple opposing forces as information.*" When I heard this I had what they probably call a revelation. Descriptions were just information. A description was not what that description described. It was merely a label for it. This was a simple enough philosophical distinction to realize, I figured. And yet descriptions are not usually thought of in this way. When you think or believe something, you think or believe a *description* of something, not that something itself. What you describe in its entirety does not jump into your head. This creates a perpetual decay on information. A clog that prevents information from changing... Eventually it so neglects describing the situation accurately that it actually hurts the situation. Oversimplification traps people in confusion over a decision that does not need to be decided. The decision itself is a stalling tactic. It is a false choice. Not merely to make you choose between two options that will both hurt you, or that are not really a choice, but in another even more profound sense. To lock you into a philosophical and linguistic framework in which all emergent thought and technology from that foundation is caused by how incomplete the framework is. Those initial conditions determine that our subsequent history will be flawed in the ways that it is flawed. All complex thought and technology is based on language. Our language trapped itself when it created opposites, even though at the same time opposites are very useful for many things. These uses caused people to set about framing as much as they could in the format of opposites, many times describing words & concepts as opposites even when it was not applicable. Simplicity generates more confusion than you think complexity does. Your degree of simplicity determines your degree of conflict. The more simple your language, the more conflict you will get into. This was the first time I had thought that getting into conflicts could have functional advantages. *"No, this is not the first time you thought of that. You had used that relationship in many ways your first time around. You need to remember them so that this time you're even better at using that relationship in even newer ways. Because last time, your ways were not new enough."* Everybody here knew me better than I knew myself.

8

I knew that many people were waiting for me to come back. But I knew that when I did, many would not believe it. Especially since what I would have to tell them would at many points be entirely against what they had been indoctrinated to believe for over a thousand years. That's a long time of psychological momentum to reverse. I also knew that most institutions of worship would not appreciate what I had to say upon return because my words would threaten the legitimacy and therefore the continuation of their existence. Since I left they had become the most powerful institutions on earth. They ruled a good proportion of the world. It is my questioning of this rule that would have the most irate response. I had to prepare for this. They were not the only institutional framework that I am destined to dismantle, but they would surely question why I, the very symbol of their belief and therefore their rule, would question and try to end it.

Other than the similarities to my opposition to the Roman Empire in my previous chance I guess. But how could they see their churches as representations of that kind of power, no matter what the denomination? People could never see similarities between institutional bureaucracies when it applied to *their* institutional bureaucracies. They didn't call them that of course, but that's what they were. People would identify with a book, a god character, or a ritual, not often realizing the system of power that was using this fancy imagery to disguise itself. When people supported a god, they weren't really supporting a god. That 'god' was the most deceptive of all lies, hiding the real purpose of growing a bureaucratic institution that's misrepresenting itself as a god. What heresy. And *it* was usually the entity throwing the accusation of heresy around. Usually because accusation and the subsequent fear of accusation breeds power... and that's the only thing an institutional bureaucracy pursues. More growth, more resources... the damned thing's an authority-generating machine.

"Seek out the zealots." Blake and I heard a voice say off in the distance. *"They are the hand of god."* We could not detect where this voice was coming from, but it sounded like it was from a great distance away, which on this scale sounded like the words themselves were echoing thunderstorms coming over the area at over a hundred miles per hour in quick repetitive waves. Hearing and feeling that didn't blow Us over, but it was very annoying on the senses. As we looked around trying to figure out what was going on, it continued to blast, *"They do as they're told, even over long time-spans."* Blake and I finally saw a curtain hanging in thin air amidst the mystical looking environment we were traveling through. From behind it stepped out a familiar laughing face, it was Benjamin. *"Sorry about the Oz effects. I just can't get enough of corrupt authority metaphors."* Blake and I laughed and welcomed him, as if we knew where we were, or somehow had dominion over the place, as if it was a home of some sort. We were just passing through, but places here had that effect on your psyche, and it felt good to run with it.

"You must steer them away from their current path." "Who?" I asked. *"Christian fundamentalists of course. Who did you think?"* "What path?" I continued to question for more detail. *"The path of fate that religious fundamentalists are currently on. You will probably only be able to help the Christian fundamentalists, because other religion's zealots will not think of you as a source of legitimate information. You're just another charlatan to them. They have their own saviors and prophets that they hold dear, people that Christian zealots consider charlatans. You're all charlatans. People just get stuck having to believe in one fake over another... for more practical rea-*

sons. Practical reasons that are lies... There is no real need to believe in a fake authority, this only inhibits growth, although this is currently not thought of in that way." "Thanks." I told Benjamin. I appreciate honesty even when painfully critical. Although at first it seems to hurt, it really helps a lot. The amount of emotional pain comes from the depth of the lie, not the revealing of the lie.

"They are waiting for you. They are actively trying to construct events to quicken your return. They are becoming increasingly impatient. They so want your return that they would sacrifice themselves to guarantee it. Sound familiar? They must've gotten such a stupid idea from you." "Probably." I told him. I might as well start admitting it. It was crossing my mind that being a Messiah produced a negative effect, even though all stories of them as characters claimed the opposite would occur. And I was going to go back to the present claiming to be Him again. "Why am I to go back to earth as the Messiah?" *"Don't claim to be the Messiah! Didn't you ever see Monty Python's: The Life of Brian? Watch it. Although it is thought of as a comedy, it is the closest representation of what historical reality was like at that time, that art has ever produced."* "I don't really understand." I told him. He sighed and said, *"You are just to step in their way. Remember, they're fundamentalists. They will think what they're told to think by their authoritarian leaders. Step in the way of their leaders. Not because they will be better able to prove that you're the Messiah -- they will easily make up whatever they have to -- but because they are already looking for someone to fill that role in their prophetic intentions. They're looking for someone to step in those shoes."*

Blake jumped in. *"If they don't believe you're the Messiah, they'll believe you're the anti-Christ. We're comfortable with them perceiving you as either. Both are remarkably similar when you think about it. Opposites often are."* Blake was a wise man. *"You know why that hap-*

pens?" Blake immediately asked. "Not enough, I suppose." I said. *"Because opposites condense a huge amount of information into two opposing positions. Simplicity sucks."*

Benjamin grabbed Blake's shoulder and stepped in front of him again. His words pierced with the knowledge of the inherent self-destruction within all of us. *"You think prophecies are written just to religiously inspire crazy people that have obsessions with coincidences? Prophecies have many reasons, like all things in nature. The most dominant reason for prophecy is the desire, of the institutional religious power at whatever time, in charge of writing and/or including it in whatever holy book, to bring that prophecy about in the future. Not for the prophecy to just happen by chance or act of god... it is written so that future zealots will make it happen! When it is most needed. It is insurance for the future in case your religion or society has failed or is oppressed by another more powerful one. Prophecy is the plan for attack to regain control. Or to take total control... The prophetic texts, no matter the religion, refer to a time of trial, of hardship, of war, of subjugation to other peoples. So that when this happens throughout the future of their history the 'faithful' can act with a plan of quite literally biblical proportions. Fate within societies is made real by the free will of the most manipulative people. Prophecies are not fulfilled by god, they are intentionally fulfilled by religious zealots with particular political goals in mind. And the writers of any prophecies know that!*

It's not aimed at mystical crazies, but at rational moderates. When the majority of a society or a religion needs to compete with another dominant society or religion, it has to have a practical game-plan. And when you're significantly weaker than those oppressing you, you have to pull God out of the playbook! What could better help you to achieve parity with your enemies than God? It's sort of a last resort plan. When everything else has failed. The rational moderates know it's bullshit, but they'll use other peoples' beliefs in bullshit to their advantage! And if there's one thing you can guarantee that the majority of people in every society still fears, it's God!"

Benjamin waved his hand in a particularly interesting pattern through the air in front of him. *"Talk to my friend Michel about it. He knows."* When Benjamin spoke his name, this man immediately appeared before us, as if he walked right through a door that wasn't there. And then Benjamin disappeared, as if he left through that same door. This man, Michel, fit the classic image of a seer, long beard 'n all. He played the role of wise elder in appearance quite well. He was the most famous of all those that predicted the future. When he began to speak, there was much guilt in his sound wave patterns. *"I am a fraud."* Those were his first words, really. I was pleased to see once again how openly forthcoming people were here. *"I took advantage of people's simple minds. I am truly sorry."* I felt that he meant it. But it was what he said next that made me understand why he had done what he had done. *"I worked for the French government. I worked for a few different European institutions, including the Catholic Church. In my time, if you didn't serve the authority, the authority served you on a plate. I didn't really want to do what I did. I felt pressure from very violent people. I did what I did because I was afraid."* I could easily understand how he felt. Authority usually had this effect on people. He continued, *"Prophecies are written with cryptic correlations & esoteric references. This is most often thought to be a means of protection from church persecution for occult practices. If people can't definitively say you wrote something heretical, it is harder to find you guilty of that crime. But that's really only part of the reason. Another part is that it makes my prophecies easier to be melded into whatever events really happen later in time, as if I was close enough. People always had a tendency to respect events that were 'close enough' in similarity. The most important reason however, was really to pre-write the future. Don't forget, most prophecies are written by institutions of religion, not in opposition to them.*" I asked him to explain further, because Benjamin's words had made me very interested in Michel's techniques of trickery.

"*Well, I'm not a fraud in the way people usually think I am. Sure, I made most of the prophecies up, spuriously calculating them based on almanacs and history books. But I was not making them up merely for notoriety or believers. Nor was I merely making money, although I made a shitload. I was working for authorities that wanted these things said. Authorities that had plans for the future, and wanted a dynamical hole dug for later generations to fall into and so direct their perception towards.*" I understood how this worked. To take one of Michel's examples, when he supposedly predicted seeing a Pope years before some man was Pope. Literature of this nature guaranteed notoriety for that Pope when he was later selected. What better PR is there? You had been predicted to be what you had become. What a spectacular way to enhance the perception of your authority. It must be god's will. It must be right for him to be Pope. It was foretold. When the whole time, it was really only an authority forcing a respected seer/quack to create the prophecy in order to give a false respect and authority to this Pope when he was later selected. Who was going to question this Pope's rule? How could they? Unless of course they knew what Michel had admitted to us today. Which they didn't...

"*Is it a promise, a plan, or a prophecy? Or are all of these things the same thing phrased for different lengths of time?*" With these quite extraordinary final words, Michel's physical image disintegrated into nothing. He was no longer standing there.

The sun was rising, which now looked as if it were 7 interconnected suns. A new day promised that we could make whatever we want happen. And what we wanted to happen was to unmake what other people were ignorantly making happen. Blake and I sat on a dune and watched the amazing display of energy in the sky, thinking about what events lay ahead. *"What do you think?"* Blake asked. "I think that last time I was on earth I was executed because I wanted to be executed." I told him. "I think that if I wasn't a martyr, none of my message would have gotten out there. The religion we were beginning would have never continued. The whole thing rested on that one event of sacrifice and standing up for one's beliefs. At the time I thought I couldn't have accomplished what I wanted to accomplish if I didn't die to climax the story and set the example. It was a more simple time. People needed violence to learn. They needed violence to accept change. That is no longer the case." He looked me stern in the face and said, *"Well done."*

9

Blake and I walked into a garden we had never seen, even on this scale. It looked perfect in every way, although we could see that that was an illusion. It was in actuality much more imperfect than any we had previously witnessed, just in very subtle ways that were unrecognizable to the simple of mind. We saw four rivers, all headed out in different directions, with busted signs next to the outgoing flow of each, naming them. When we walked closer, we saw that two of the signs had names that were still somewhat legible. They read *Tigris & Euphrates*. At this point we both laughed at how ridiculously strange & obvious this particular experience was. In an instant, a woman appeared before us. She was quite literally the most attractive woman we had ever seen, in ways very difficult to describe, she was seemingly imperfect to infinite degrees. And she was completely naked. She had no sign of embarrassment or discomfort or awkwardness. She literally acted as if she wasn't naked, but also as if, if you felt uncomfortable, you were the only one who should be embarrassed. Insecurities of others did not affect her negatively.

The first thing she said was an assertively stated question. *"Blake, will you make love to me now?"* Blake did not hesitate. They had sex right there on the ground of this garden, in front of me. I sat watching on the edge of the Tigris, very interested in the direct freedom of her will. It was not offensive to them that I watched, as I was most respectful of the natural necessity of their actions. When they were done (*for the time*) rolling around under what looked like to me familiar trees, we began to talk. Blake was glowing with reflective iterations of himself. I asked her what her name was. *"I'm Eve, of course."* I immediately jumped to the next question, asking her if this was really the Garden of Eden. *"No. Of course not... Entirely too predictable, still you are. Similarity does not ever mean total similarity. Haven't you picked that up yet?"* Blake and her sitting there naked laughing at me, was very funny to me. *"I'm sorry, I'm just giving you a little hell because you not only come from a sexually repressive society, you helped to create a lot of them as well. I would've asked you to join us, but I knew you wouldn't."* She said. Shyness is the real bitch.

She was supposedly the first woman on earth, but she did not see it that way. *"I'm a representation of something that's impossible to happen. Again, a good story, **if** you know it's not real. Who would really believe that things in nature start with only one entity, then inexplicably two entities, and then spawn forth linearly from there?"* "The simple of mind", I said. *"Exactly."* She said. Blake sat there the whole time nearly incapable of saying anything (*except Catherine, and how she will love sharing in this experience*), his smile so broad, his feelings and perception so intensely stimulated. Eve continued, *"You know even if anyone was to claim any of this (and they still do, especially where you're going), you would have to correct them. In fact where you're going, you're going to need to do a lot of correcting. Through experiment of course... We don't need you fucking up again!"* We all laughed. *"You're going to try to transform societies on a worldwide basis, without imposing your will. Science will help you do that. But you will have to be very careful. There are some things you'll need to ask people to test via experiment that will be very difficult for them to achieve emotionally. But it is very necessary for their future survival. Life within society is now too complex to be scientifically ignored."* I asked her where the snake was.

"He's busy planning. There's a lot for you to do, you know. You don't have to worry about what he's doing now. He, like you, is rectifying a situation he intentionally left unresolved. When he told me in the story that we would

not surely die (even though god said that we would), he &
god knew why he was right. He intended to help us avoid
the inherent perils of perception later. It wasn't his fault
the humans did what they did, and it wasn't really their
fault either (nor god's). The snake was just foreshadowing
it a little. He was letting them know that when they needed
him later, he would be there to help." Then she very
abruptly steered the conversation elsewhere. *"You know*
why men rule the world?" I told her I didn't but that that
sort of information might help me upon returning to earth.
"More than you could ever know, I'm sure." She said. *"Pa-*
triarchal society is almost entirely derivative of a sexually
repressive society. Women can easily handle a certain pe-
riod without sex, should circumstance force it. When men
are prevented from having sex though, their chemicals re-
spond with exponentially more aggression. This excessive
aggression is what holds the inequality of male power in
place.

    No one on earth remembers the ancient transition
from matriarchal to patriarchal societies. There is no re-
cord of it, for good reason, as it was one of the first mas-
sive deceptions perpetrated on humanity. So I understand
why it persists. However, like all dynamical systems, an
iteration of an initial condition occasionally comes around
again to subtly let you know how it all could have gotten
started. In this case that circumstance is when women are
told they can achieve greater political power through with-
holding sex from their male counterparts. This was the sub-
terfuge that started it all (later locked-in to place with that
monogamous curse of marriage, that changed women to
property). This was the trick initiated by certain men who
wanted political control over all other men, and all women.
They somehow convinced the women in power at the time
that they could get more power by preventing men from
having sex, rather than their current methods of near con-
stant sex. The method of frequent sex had already proven to

be very effective. But people with power always tend to want more, and they fall for tricks sometimes in pursuit of more.

What women can realize again, to take back the power they deserve, as they are much more humane and wise organizers of human beings, is the tactical benefits of tearing down sexual repression in any way they can. The easiest way to do that is to have sex with as many men as you want, as often as you can. This reverses the control of the men in power, because they rely almost entirely on sexually repressed males that respond eagerly to aggressive scenarios imposed on them because of their horribly deprived lives. There are many social norms in the present that conflict with this. It will be hard. The men that control all human beings have many layers of psychological protection against events like this returning to earth. They have fear of sex built up in people's minds heavier than fear of violence. Which is a clear sign that their initial tactic is still working. They twist concepts like honor and respect to make sex look like it's something to be preserved. They lie that there is a single purpose for sex, and that is procreation only. There are no other reasons for sex according to them, although this has been proven false. At times they have even created and/or enhanced (or delivered) diseases of a sexual nature, a form of bio-terrorism, to stop women from re-achieving their status as political equals. These certain men are ruthless and they are violent. But that is, despite all opinion to the contrary, not the only way nature wins.

When women in massive numbers once again turn the tables by actively pursuing sex without fear or loss of respect or of status or honor, even between each other (as this woman-to-woman loss of psychological standing is a reinforcing effect of male dominance), they will gain back equality. Women will once again organize together throughout the world. They will physically (via sex) force all men to behave less violently. Men are much less likely to act violently en mass if they are sexually (and therefore psychologically) healthy. If you remember anything at all, remember that sex has more than one purpose. Remember that its second most important purpose (some argue it is the first) is relief of social tension. Matriarchal societies easily develop when social tension is within a healthy (low) range. Matriarchal societies are way overdue for a return to earth. Please do what you can to make this a reality again."

"I will..." I said. It had been something I had thought about for a long time, but I had never achieved the wisdom of this description before. It filled me with a knowledge and level of love and interconnectedness of all humanity that I was not familiar with until now. This was something very new, even if originally old, I thought, and something that powerful men would resist with limitless violence and trickery in response, during the present. But I also knew we would easily be able to subvert that violence and deception if we persisted no matter what. And that these powerful men should not want to maintain the power they have, if that power was not as powerful as it could be if men were less violent and more sexual in character. Although this would have to be empirically proven to them. And like Eve said, this would be very difficult emotionally for a violent society. But it was something I was determined to try.

At the very moment I thought this she got in my face. *"This is something you've been needing to do for 2000 years. It's about god damn time!"* She took me into her and fucked the hell out of me for I don't even know how long. Despite many of my followers assuming I was a virgin because I was supposedly born of one, I had a girlfriend before... my followers just judged her vocation as inappropriate. So she wasn't written about as my girlfriend when she appeared in the story. Now any women I was with were going to be. It was like I had never lived before and then experienced the most profound mental and physical mix of experience ever felt. I had in my existence no experience remotely close to similarity with it. I felt the complexity of my perception expand beyond what I thought was possible on *any* scale. Being with her was like becoming a god. *"All you have to do is tell them what I said,"* she spoke with the softest voice I'd ever heard, *"and it will be taken care of."* I loved her, and as she had also enlightened me, I would love every woman.

10

And then god created all the animals on the earth. And He gave man dominion over them. But then again, when everyone thought about it, He didn't. We all seemed to be part of the same chain of domination. Blake and I found ourselves toiling in some field far from the garden we had just been in. We did not know how we had gotten here, but the excessive workload was fiercely irritating. We did not even really know whom we were toiling for. As soon as we recognized this irritation, Benjamin came walking up to us from out of nowhere. *"Put down those tools, and pick up these."* He tossed us each some papers with writing on them. The title on this writing was *"The Grand Pecking Order Fallacy"*. It talked about the layers of increasing complexity and differentiation in all species of life in a way I had not seen before. It first described all of the layers of life as using their level of complexity to always manipulate those thought to be below it in complexity, just because their structures held less complexity, and so those more able than others were determined to continue doing this. It said that St. Maynard had described the process as, *"This is necessary... life feeds on life feeds on life feeds on life."* I could not remember a Saint Maynard. *"This is an enlightening description"*, it said, *"but like all descriptions, it is incomplete, always missing what can be newly discovered details and more complex descriptions."*

Benjamin smiled as we read. The writing continued, *"Everything in existence (including all the biological organisms in it) becomes more complex. While nonlinear dynamics exist in nature, that does not mean a suppressive hierarchy of increasingly 'better' beings is destined or 'supposed to' harm that which is 'below it' for gain. In fact as nature becomes more complex, the more complex beings increasingly expand the range of scale to which they do not harm other beings (is your distinction line from: dogs up the chain to humans, or all animals needn't be killed – only plants, or something else?)"* Benjamin interrupted our reading. *"The crocodile eats the gazelle. The elephant eats the plants. Some animals are more ruthless than others."* I thought about which brain functions are more complex, an elephant's or a crocodile's. *"An elephant."* Benjamin said. Then I thought about which animal would win in a fight. Benjamin answered my thought, *"Crocodiles and elephants rarely if ever come into contact with each other. When they do find each other near, they're both very good at getting the other to keep their distance.*

When human beings first started developing the earliest forms of society, they looked to the animals for guidance." We start out stupid, I thought. *"Only because we had a limited knowledge of animals at the time, and perceived this limited knowledge to be absolutely complete and correct. So the societies we built were designed after the most ruthless animals. Because our ignorance at that time perceived ruthless as equal to best."* We know more about animals now, I thought. *"Yes we do."* Benjamin said this with that twirling tone that connotes further inquiry is necessary. *"In these initial stages of societal history, humans made elaborate designs of the pyramidal hierarchies that they thought represented the universe and everything in it. The animal world had its own hierarchy of better and worse. The most violent animals were seen to be the most powerful animals. This is not so. But back then when all people were intelligent enough to observe and measure was the ruthlessness of animals, I can see how they got that impression. Power to them was how big your teeth were."* That explains a lot. They must have at that point thought that they had solved the problem. And now all they had to do was keep expanding the solutions. Build bigger teeth.

"Precisely." Benjamin was pleased. Blake was chewing on a piece of crocodile meat. He started talking

with his mouth full, *"Yeah but we've got some determinism already built into our structure as human beings. This stuff tastes great!"* "Precisely," Benjamin said, pleased again. He did not seem to notice any inconsistency between Blake's and my statements. *"It all comes down to what your intelligence directs you to build... off of what you already have innately. Which pathways do you extend and which do you abandon? Selecting these paths, determines your fate. Don't forget that paths of fate repeat what has already happened in the path before, at irregular intervals."* This made me think that I heard this sort of idea somewhere before. *"So I should look out for crocodiles."* Blake said laughing. Benjamin smiled and said, *"Not necessarily. Events in the world occur nonlinearly. What some humans call Karma, does not happen so directly. Causality is a very big thing."* This made me think that the natural drive toward equality and justice and the strong laws of statistics emerged from the same thing in nature. Or were they the same thing occurring in different situations?

Benjamin continued, *"As intelligence increases, ruthlessness decreases. If consciousness does not increasingly lower its violence relative to beings on its scale, it increasingly risks destroying itself."* Because of random mutation in natural selection, I thought, simpler life forms than us will still hold many valuable techniques and survival properties that we don't have. So no layer of complexity is better than that which is simpler than it. All have randomly distributed survival-value properties, despite also having differing degrees of complexity. *"Therefore viewing all of life in the model of a hierarchy is very mistaken."* Benjamin said as he smiled again. He then held out his hands as far as they could stretch. *"To do so ignores the majority of valuable adaptive survival traits. It renders your species doomed."* We must have thought hierarchies were very good models to describe nature with. *"They may be good, but like every description they are incomplete and should be expanded or abandoned for better methods of describing. When those new methods are figured out."* Now we had a newer method. No life is below any other. All life forms are more or less complex than each other. But all layers of complexity hold potential benefits to all other layers. So while certain life forms are more complex than others, all hold the same random adaptive trait value.

11

Although prophecy was everything that I had previously learned it to be, some experimentally verifiable dynamical information was also put in to increase its supposed validity. To this day (*for some reason – likely ethnocentrism*), most people did not understand how ancient peoples attained this information. Information such as that the distant future would hold an increase in wars and disease and population and knowledge, etc… Essentially this "mystical" information was merely the known demographic data of the time, input in religious texts as if the bible, amongst other things, was an almanac. Thinkers in 2000 BC saw that the number of nations constantly increased as population expanded and new territory was settled. This was one of many quite simple mathematical realizations. So, even at that early time, it was known that thousands of years from their time, the world's population would be huge, many nations would've developed and spawned off of previous nations, and those nations would likely perpetually fight wars with each other. After all, nations in their time did those things. There would be much more of everything that was happening in their day. They saw the progressive expansion of knowledge just as easily. They knew that after thousands of years, what they saw to already be an exponential growth process would be at an incredibly complex state. In 2000 BC, very rational people could roughly measure the growth of population, knowledge, technology, war and destructive capability. Thousands of years into the future… Of course they did these measurements amidst a mystical framework that granted more respect to their religions. But they were relatively good measurements.

Change was always going to happen faster and on a larger scale the further into the future history went. People were often ignorant and so unprepared for this nearly every time thus far. So when change happened in the beginning of the twenty-first century, it would be woefully large and uncontrollably damaging. When change happens, it tends to be violent. But this is not because of change. It is because we have not developed and so could not implement the knowledge of fluidly directing this increasing amount of change. Change, as it increases in magnitude, can be directed peacefully (*fluidly*). This rarely happened only because of our unscientific understanding of it. We were living it, so change was much more susceptible to a mystical framework. This was dangerous. As ancient peoples hypothesized what would happen in this future worldwide change, they saw an ultimate destruction as unavoidable.

As I had thought, change occurs violently only when people do not accept the new pathways these changes open. It is the fault of our collective misunderstanding. Ancient peoples must also have seen this circumstance long ago. They couldn't have seen it as clearly as we can now though. It will be very difficult for enough of the world's population to reverse their traditional views enough to allow for new pathways to direct the magnitude of change into the future fluidly. There are too many people that will not budge. Subconsciously, they want the violence. The violence validates their traditional worldview. Resisting change has become quite the fad through the millennia. This resistant worldview would obviously also change after an end of the world scale disaster. But our job was to insure that such a revelation happened before an apocalyptic event and thus prevented any unnecessary violence. The pressure was building. And as the 'dam broke', so to speak, there would only be more validation of this self-destructive pattern. I was not sure exactly how we were going to redirect this changeable determinism, but I had the feeling we had more than enough capability to do so. With everything I'd seen, there was no doubt. And I was told all I'd have to do was convey what I'd seen. Communication of ideas was somehow all that was necessary. The means to implement the ideas were already entrenched in the worldwide network of organization.

I had been walking as I was thinking. As I thought these things the paths upon which I walked diverged constantly. There was an option to go left and right nearly every other step, either way curving in different directions after that. Each new path containing more new offshoot paths than the path they originally branched from. Direction itself seemed to be expanding, although I thought this was somewhat confusing at the time. I became all the more confused as I began taking more and more paths, even as they branched. Somehow I was able to occupy multiple directions at once. And the more I walked, the more directions I could simultaneously pursue. Surprisingly, after some time of advancing these motions in every conceivable direction, I came to just one large door. Above the door was written: *Is it strange that things naturally gravitate toward their interest? How far does one perceive themselves?*

12

"*Welcome back.*" It said. "I'm back?" I said without thinking. I responded without even knowing whom I was responding to. It didn't feel any different to me here. And I guess I was too used to speaking when prompted, before thinking about what I would say. I must've picked up my own little submission to authority conditioned response somewhere. "*Probably from me.*" It said. "*Sorry about that. But it's the simplistic way things were done back then.*" I looked around. I was standing in the middle of a very thick jungle. Plants all over the place, I barely had space to move around. I felt a hand reach out to mine, although I could not see the hand. The hand directed me into a clearing. There was still a dense amount of life around, but there was enough space to not feel strangled by it. I still could not see the hand, nor that which the hand was attached to, although I was quite sure that I had been directed to where I was via someone's physical form.

I stood before what looked like the stage of the beginning of life. I could see more species interacting and emerging from here than any place I had been to on earth before. It was constantly expanding. Each organism building on the previous chances… Each individual creation re-creating mutated forms of itself… It spoke again. "*My son. How disappointed I've become with you. All of you.*" I sensed it looking around although I could not see it doing this. "Father?" I ignorantly threw out there. "*Sure. If that's what you want to call me.*" "I don't understand." I think I said I don't understand a few times actually. "*You don't need to understand. Stop worrying about it. It will only prevent you from understanding what's really necessary.*" "I don't understand that either, thanks for being so vague." I could sense it smiling somehow. "*I'm still learning too, you know. All of us are always pursuing more beneficial methods of interaction. It is what we are.*"

"Is this Eden?" I asked. "*So obsessed with similarity, with the familiar.*" It seemed to sigh. "*It's the closest thing to it that ever really existed. This is the likely original location where humans developed as a biological species... the origin. It's possible at least. There's still debate about that here. Let's just say this might be the sort of place that story was describing. But actually, the story described a specific area circling the Persian Gulf. We are in what the powerful people in the present call the Democratic Republic of the Congo. We are in the center of what they call Africa.*" I sensed it pointing somewhere, even though I could not see any finger. I still looked in the correct direction. I saw small monkeys shuffling around in the clearing. They looked like chimpanzees. They were jumping and shouting and eating plants and performing other behaviors that chimpanzees normally do. "*They are bonobos.*" It said. Then it said, "*Watch.*" As it said this, the chimpanzees got up on two legs and walked around as if they were human. I was astonished. "*Watch.*" It said again. As they walked around, they picked up rocks and sticks and used them as tools. They dragged the sticks together to form more complex structures out of them that had functional uses. They were still simple tools, but these were behaviors I did not know existed in animals other than humans.

"*They hedge my bet. They will replace you, if you fail. That is, if you do not destroy them in the process of failing. In which case, it will take a long time before consciousness expands here again. And if you don't mind, I would prefer not waiting.*" "Is this real? Are we on earth? Or are we still on a more complex time-scale of earth?" I was having trouble understanding what and where I was witnessing. "*Yes. This is earth in the present. I have brought you backwards through the scales, as has been prophesied.*" It continued to speak, but with more intensity.

"Humans will have to adapt in new ways. In order to survive, you will have to adapt collectively within your lifetimes. Despite their simplicity, these animals have a skill humans don't have, and humans will need to learn that skill." "What could be so important?" I asked… it must know how much I don't know, so it didn't seem upset with my many questions.

"Watch." The voice said again. When I looked, I saw two of the chimps get angry with each other. They began to position themselves to fight, yelling at each other. After this the most unexpected thing happened. They grabbed each other and had sex with each other. Right there. They held each other with compassion as relative equals. It was consensual. There was seemingly no dominance about it. And because monkey sex is quick, it was over a few seconds after it began. Their fight had been resolved. "What the hell is this all about?" I asked it, very frustrated and confused. *"It is their skill."* "A little more detail please…" I pleaded. *"Eve told you about it. Sex has more than one main purpose. Another main purpose is the relief of social tension. To prevent violence."* I was stunned thinking about it. I had never heard of these animals before, and I had never seen anything like the behavior they exhibited. Even when Eve told me about it in humans, I did not know that another species on earth was currently doing it.

It then abruptly changed the subject. *"There's a lot you don't know about Eve as well. She is one of the most powerful women in the history of human literature. Men were sure to try to demonize her. Your followers demonized her to the nth degree… they found they could rally support by suppressing women through making Eve look like the responsible party for all human sin. I say sin, but you and I both know that sin doesn't exist. Sin is also merely a description. A description of a collection of behaviors… Behaviors that have both positive and negative consequences depending on the particular circumstances in which those behaviors take place... Sin is just another too-simplistic description. So if I was you, and in the minds of most of your followers I am, I'd stop using it to describe things."* "I'll take your word for it." I told it. *"No. Stop doing that too. Don't take anyone's word for anything. I thought you realized this already. You have to test things. You have to stop believing things. Even what I'm saying right now... If you believe what I'm saying, you will fail. You will all fail. You have to repeatedly test the validity of everything that is said. And this becomes very difficult through time, because more and more things are said. It seems like there's not enough time to test it all. But there is. Make time."*

I had a lot to test already. Apparently everyone did. But it had assured me that there would be more time available increasingly into the future so that this could be done. I was caught up in thought about what it had already said, but it wasn't done speaking yet. It seemed like it had been waiting a long time to say all these things. What it said next, made me feel like I had betrayed it in my first life. *"With the first few commandments, I thought I clearly put the impression in your head that 'nothing is better than god'. As in, do not worship or believe in any other gods, do not make representations of me (idols), etc. But you missed the larger point of what I was saying. This means, no depictions of god. Even saying or writing the word itself describes it too much. It does not mean replace god with nothing. It means... Do not describe me. When you describe me, you destroy me, and then you destroy each other. You should not believe in any descriptions of god. They are blasphemous (if you believe in that sorta thing). Descriptions break the 1ˢᵗ few commandments. Even the 1ˢᵗ few commandments themselves violate the 1ˢᵗ few commandments somewhat because they are descriptions of what god wants, and no one who writes can know that. That is not to say that the sayings (the 1ˢᵗ few commandments) themselves do not have enormous value. Those that*

fake descriptions of what god thinks sometimes have pro-
foundly wise things to say. It's just cooler when they admit
it. And when they don't use it to control people (especially
when those people are killed in the process)."

It then again abruptly changed the subject. "*It is*
known here now that the universe has no edge and it has no
center. This description is better than they've ever known it
before. It is much more useful than those before it, but it is
a spatial description. A temporal-spatial description sus-
pects that the accelerated unfolding sequence of time is it-
self an edge of the universe… and that a center of the uni-
verse, is now." If there was one thing I understood about
this voice, it was that it was very confusing and complicated. I couldn't help but wonder if it was doing that on
purpose. "*Stop worrying so much. But never stop question-*
ing. You've got a lot to do now that you've been infused
back into the now." "So I'm really back in the unfolding
present now?" "*Yes.*" It said. "*Today is December 25th,*
2006 to them. I thought you'd get a kick out of that."

13

The earth in the present looked just as I had remembered it my first time around. The only difference I noticed was the patterns of cloud formations. Everything else looked very much the same. Although I was back in what people called reality now, I was still able to communicate with the other minds from the scales of complexity beyond the present. I would still need their help, I was told. They were all as much a part of what I was doing as I was, I was told. And I wasn't just told this... I had seen it proven again and again. I was not alone in this exercise. So it was time for us to get started. I walked and climbed and swam west following the river across the unbelievable landscape of this Congo until I got to what on earth today they call a city within what they call a nation-state. I think they called things cities only because they had a lot of people and technological capabilities packed into a tight area. I took a flight from this city of Kinshasa, to the United States. I had to go to the United States. This place was the center of all power on earth in the present. This was where I could have the most effect.

Of all the places in the United States I could've flown into, I decided I needed to start in Washington D.C. The culture shock of two thousand years of history was getting to me, even though I had been briefed on history's developments since my time. Living that kind of transition is something that cannot ever be sufficiently prepared for. Almost immediately I needed help, and almost immediately another mind came to my rescue from the temporal plane above the present. Just seeing the inequality discrepancy in life experience between where I had just been in Africa and where I now was in the United States was emotionally devastating. I began to think it was too late. Humans had already stretched the inequality too far to recover. I was im-

mediately questioning my ability to do anything. Martin
came to my rescue. He guided me through the traffic of
gawkers on every street corner over to the Capitol building.
I guess Martin knew something about the comforting ability of familiarity. When switching between time scales, familiarity was even more important to establish for comfort
and sanity than it was within any particular time scale.
Martin pretty much had to drag me by the time we got
close. I was so tired. This must've looked very strange to
people around, because Martin was not visible to them.
Eventually he helped me get to the very same steps I had
been on with Benjamin & Burrhus on the time scale above
the present. In this position I felt extraordinarily better.
Almost instantly... It was remarkable. The view of the
Capitol building itself on this scale was so funny; so much
a shell of what it was where I had been before.

"Notice the differences." Martin told me. *"They will
help you understand much about this place."* First of all, I
thought, Benjamin & Burrhus were not here, nor was anyone playing chess outside anywhere around here. Of course
there was just one building, not the many iterations of the
same building I had seen before. Things repeated less on
this scale. And their repetitions moved smaller and therefore harder to see on a much steeper curve than they did
where I last was. So the only repetitions of the Capitol
building I saw around the building itself were the pictures
of it on the fifty-dollar bills in most people's pockets. Martin asked me, *"What do you think of it? Is it worth sav-
ing?"* I immediately answered, "Of course, yes." At this
point another man came walking down the steps carrying a
little table. He set the table down in the same position it had
been in when/where Benjamin and Burrhus were and said,
"Correct answer." It was Malcolm. It had been a while
since I had seen him too. I hadn't recognized him. No one
in the present could see either of them, but I sat for hours

on the steps watching them play chess on the little table Malcolm had brought down.

"*Europe had the advantage in recent history of only a set of initial conditions. It is always an almost entirely geographically based advantage. Soon another region will hold the advantage, as the Middle East did prior to Europe. As Africa did prior to the Middle East... I suspect it will be South America next.*" Malcolm had been flying far through the scales prior to being stuck with everyone else just above the present. I thought about why regional advantages shift through time. "*That would be mostly the result of the changing climate.*" He said. "*Every couple thousand years or so the unfair advantages given to a certain region move to another region. The Sahara desert was as green as Europe in 6000 BC you know. There just wasn't nearly enough people alive yet to build large societies.*" By the time there were enough people born and collected in certain areas to exploit the advantages, I thought, the geographical & climate advantages were mostly in the Middle East, Asia and Europe. "*Sure, that's an accurate enough statement for now.*" "And then eventually enough people collected together in these places to exploit their surroundings by building societies there." "*Somewhat, yes.*" Malcolm said. "*Then, a couple thousand years after your original time, so many people encompassed so much of the earth that something very interesting happened.*" "What's that?" "*Climate change happens faster when there are enough people concentrated in societies exploiting these unfair advantages. So if some societies end up doing very well at the expense of all others, nature speeds up the process of shifting the advantages to someone else. The earth has a sort of built in immune system for over-exploitation. Because when people exploit each other, it is obviously also the case that they are actively exploiting the earth and its resources as well.*" "So any society given the advantage is determined to destroy the environment and its neighbors, allowing other societies to try to attempt to create a cleaner, better industry when that advantage shifts." *"Yeah, sort of... You're close enough I guess."*

He was telling me that it's not really just chance operating amidst all the motion on earth. (*If it were that way things would equal out faster and more often.*) There are pockets of chaotic dynamics that allow for severely unfair relationships to exist for certain periods of time. But then the extremely unfair advantage itself moves to another area, eventually balancing into a more complex chance. This made me think about how rulers of nations thought they could hold their unfair advantages indefinitely into the future. Forever. Martin responded to my thought, *"Stubborn, aren't they? They fight against their own interest. But they do not know that yet. They see holding the unfair advantages forever as their interest. This is part of why you are here now."* I could sense why they would see the world in this way. Must've been their perceptual myopia acting up again. Probably largely because of the over-simplistic descriptions they were using. Some of those simple descriptions were ones I had given them to use. And I had called those descriptions truth. Nearly every moment I seemed to notice more and more aspects of how I had made this world a worse place.

"Don't be so hard on yourself. We're going to need you to be confident again." Martin was a good man. He was one of the nicest and wisest to ever walk the face of the earth. I had been told this by almost everyone that had ever been on earth. Martin had the reputation everyone usually ascribed to me. He was much more deserving of it. *"America is near a turning point."* He said. *"What those alive there now do with their time will lock-in either a great idea or a great tragedy for the future. The great tragedy has an early head start."* Here comes more pressure, I thought. *"And both the idea and the tragedy will think they are great in the present. But the idea will show itself with its inde-*

pendence. The idea will show unparalleled independence and freedom, while the tragedy will tend toward the opposite of freedom while using the word freedom to move against it. That is how people will know which is which.'' "You say the tragedy has a head start already? Is there a way to still catch up?" *"There is still time. But all must move quickly. And all must remember to always move nonviolently. At that point time will move with you, and no head start can outpace you then.''* We could always be faster than them. They were so used to being violent. *"Human freedom is the most important thing there is on the earth. Make sure she is protected from her domestic enemies, for they are already knocking her down.''* I left Washington D.C. and headed north.

14

"All formal dogmatic religions are fallacious and must never be accepted by self-respecting persons as final." She broke the mirrors because they distort. I could see her mentally from afar, and could hear her well. When she spoke, hilarious wisdom emerged. Hypatia knew authority well. She had experienced it first hand, like I had. With less official pronouncement though... Her mind was silenced via a vicious mob of henchmen. It was business as usual for the all too familiar 'vocal opponents to authority' loop. Her opposition wasn't even that big of a deal. The situation of unresolved conflict itself could've been handled in so many different ways. Had people cared to think about any other options, that is. Authority responds quickly. Not because it thinks fast, but because it doesn't think.

"Reserve your right to think, for even to think wrongly is better than not to think at all. Thoughts that prove incorrect when tested with experiments in reality are easily changed. Reserve your right to be proven wrong. It's better than being proven right because so much growth can come of it. Being wrong is only stupid when you stay wrong after you have seen your position proven wrong." Arguing was always the solution to her, and I understood why that was so important now. It wasn't that she loved the drama or the ordeal or the confrontation, it was that she consistently wanted to more fluidly manage the inevitable influx of con- flicting positions. This achieved greater growth, and more thought for all. This brought solutions rather than avoiding the increasing pileup of conflict that would build until an eventual avalanche brought something truly horrible into existence. It was at this moment that I felt a profound pres- ence I had not felt in a very long time. The force of reckon- ing knocked me to the ground and I melted into the soil, somewhat disrupting the vision I had been experiencing of

one of the women I love. Someone had entered the fold of this realm, and I knew who it was, I had been waiting for him since I got back. It was written that we should meet for this final battle, but I didn't expect it to be before I knew more.

"*Listen to her. She knows what she is talking about,*" was the first thing he said. So I regained my connection with her speech, out of respect for her not compliance to him. Hypatia sung, "*To teach superstitions as truth is a most terrible thing.*" To which he began ranting immediately, "*I agree. I don't even fucking exist. And I don't say that in some philosophical sense... I am not a real entity. I am a fictitious character. I am a superstition. I am a storybook villain made up to provide nonexistent aversive consequences so that your behavior is conditioned to the likes of people such as Burrhus. You must be hallucinating me right now.*" I asked him assertively "I know what you are, but you're still gonna help me, right?" His terse response was "*Sure.*" We weren't used to working together, but that was a significant mistake we had both made repeatedly years ago that we were willing to change.

Apparently since then he had just been hanging out here the whole time doing nothing... waiting for me I guess. He assured me with a grin that he had been having the most fun an entity can possibly have on this scale. I stared him back with the certainty that would convey the assurance of my respect for his appreciation of the finer things in strife. The first thing he asked me was, "*You hear who the pope is now?*" I didn't have to inform him that I just got back and I had not yet been briefed about many of the details of our mission. Pope John Paul II had been one of the most respected people to occupy the office (it's a steep challenge to avoid not becoming a monster when you sit in the pope's institutional chair, and J.P. did better than most). But apparently, from what my new partner was saying, the new guy had no hesitation unleashing his claws.

"It's the Ratz! I've been laughing my ass off ever since he got in there. I knew right away when he was picked that the decision had been made to go ahead with plan B. That the epitome of supposedly intelligent civilization was giving up! That you were coming back." Enthusiasm and attention to complexity were strong points for him. He was in the details.

I didn't have to ask him what *plan B* was, he was already about to tell me. *"It's the plan to make the end of the world! To actually make what the majority of people on earth think the end of the world is... a reality. To make it happen! On purpose! What idiots! Hahaha! It would never have happened on its own. Humans want to make it come about! Western civilization is willing to risk its ass on intentionally fulfilling a prophecy! It is not that many societies haven't used this built in function of prophecy before... this is just the most recent and the ultimate of its horrible occurrences! Bureaucracy building has finally achieved its pinnacle of stupidity. The 'Middle Eastern' governments and the 'Western' governments are more than happy to be artificially unified against each other for the purpose of expanding & competing for power on a level that has never before been attempted! Humans still need mass violence to organize alliances and more complex institutional networks of bureaucracies! Your father must've damned them! Hah! The world's two most powerful religions going head to head in a match for the other 4 billion minds they don't already have under their spell! And it's not that they're competing with each other mostly either. They each already have a billion minds, and they know fighting each other amidst the game board of the entire world will force all the others to take a side! It's brilliant in its assholishness! On average Islam & Christianity should gain control of about 2 billion more people each!"*

The unparalleled anger and infinite opposition I felt to this plan was immediate. It was in fact a main part of why I was back on earth. I knew that he didn't support the plan, even though most people would assume that the entity with his name and his position would've been the architect of such a plan. I think his sarcastic description of it was for effect and showed if anything an equally opposing position to it as mine. We were, after all, in an alliance to stop it from happening. And alliance formation was the primary tool behind *plan B*. We were of course much better at it than they were though. But people didn't know that. They were too wrapped up in their own arrogance at the discovery of such important knowledge. They jumped at the chance to use it when the initial formalities had been worked out. Impatience is a form of stupidity. I'm sure the creators of the new sciences involved in this endeavor were aware of the ignorant people they were handing that technology over to. But what could they do? These scientists were at the top of their fields, and these politicians were at the top of theirs. The current order did not allow the scientists to direct the policy this technology would be used in. The ignorant power brokers were in charge. They were people who would never have developed the science on their own, and yet they were the ultimate authority in using it. The whole structure of this order seemed so clearly oversimplistic, and we laughed again at humanity's propensity for fucking itself.

"*This is going to be fun.*" He could easily say that. He was used to this sort of shit. And I had an unequal share of the responsibility.

15

The next day I asked Satan to get ahold of Burrhus. I wanted to ask him more about how & why *he* thought the structures of human society were so simple. Satan walked outside and walked back inside with him in less than ten seconds. How convenient, except that Burrhus looked pissed. He would surely be his usual distracting, deceptive, irritated self. He began by randomly yelling, *"Look at all the ethnocentrism & racism in books that mostly have 'white' main characters, and they're mostly men, to appeal to an ignorant audience that can only appreciate a story if characters within it look like them (or look like the promoted epitome of what their society wants its citizens to be) and/or share the same beliefs as them."* I needed clarification. But I followed his tangent nonetheless. I threw out a response just short enough that it wouldn't make a person start coughing from saying too much. "These class, race, sexuality, religious, ideological, gender, familial, ethnicity, & nationality layers of our identity intentionally stratify us within a hierarchy, right?" *"The only reason for classification is to organize according to preference. Accept someone else's description of **your** identity, and you negate your existence. You accept oppression."* He said. That's what I was looking for. We can create our own identity for these subjects, our own classifications, I thought. Or at least, we need to make more layers. The simple ones we have today are not enough. And they are never good enough... we were just too ignorant to realize that in the past. We can all share ethnic traits (just by transferring/mixing our cultures & ourselves), and our species is essentially genetically the same, as race has been scientifically proven to exist only as a social construction (*a manipulative tool*). Racism exists because of this colonizing tool for dividing people by description. There are no sub-species of humans.

"But quite literally, most human beings are not yet educated enough (do not read enough) to even understand all those concepts and words, and they're too busy and proud and ignorant to look them up when they notice that they do not sufficiently understand something. So they usually agree or disagree without testing. It is not entirely their fault. It is mostly the fault of those that had the power to educate them but refused in order to better control them. I will not be the one to educate them." "Why not? You still want to control them?" *"Why not? The universe is obsessed with control."* "I don't agree. The universe in its simpler forms maybe... But not where it's been heading." *"Hierarchy still exists, does it not? Even at more complex levels?"* "Yes to some extent, but it is more refined. It works in different ways. It is nothing like hierarchies are here. Control is increasingly dissipated. Power in the present begins to take different shapes as it abandons that simple old pyramid shape for layered structures." *"So, hierarchies still exist, but they are not shaped in pyramids? There is no more top-down ordering? You think that will solve the problem?"*

"Top-down structures have by this point been demonstrated to be useful only to a certain degree. At that critical point they inhibit further growth. Their simple value prevents organizations from getting more value. In other words, they suck." *"I already know that. You had the devil pull me away from a sexual encounter with Marilyn for that?"* "Sorry, I didn't know you were busy. I didn't know he was interrupting. But he probably knew. I should have assumed he'd try to bring you here at the time it'd make you most upset." *"Everyone's always busy! No one has time for what other people think!"* Satan sat laughing in the corner. Orchestrating conflict seemed to be enjoyable for a lot of people, even when there was no more value in it than a laugh. "Look," I said to Burrhus. "I realize you enjoy controlling people. But I also think that behind your desire are rational decisions that make controlling people a valuable behavior to you. I think I've found a more valuable behavior to re-condition you with so that you enjoy this something new in the same way. But you'll behave in a better way... With even more value added." *"How do I know you're not lying to me?! I've already got a lot riding on my current behaviors! It will be hard to make me change! And besides, I set my conditions for myself!"* Or so everyone thought, I thought.

"Show me the money!" He yelled. He was interested in how new methods of non-hierarchical organizing could produce more profit. I told him I was working on that. I needed a little more time. *"You have it! You don't need my permission. Now, can I go back to what I was doing? She must be wondering where in hell I disappeared to."* Satan grabbed him and said, *"Don't worry, I've been keeping her company."* He then dragged Burrhus through the wall and they were both gone. I needed to get moving. I could sense that people were waiting for me in New York. It was much more difficult, but even on this scale I could sense some aspects of what was coming next before next was now.

I saw Emma the second I got to New York City. She was in the subway, as I had imagined she would be. Even though she couldn't be seen, because she had been dead for many decades, she was trying to block the security checkpoints that were part of what Americans were being conditioned to call 'the new normal', or 'the post Sept. 11th world'. She was crying out in opposition to the authoritarian tactics of an ignorant and therefore all too malleable police force. Submissive people, one by one, would follow each other through the checkpoints having their bodies and baggage searched for the perceived to be necessary reason of security. This upset her very much, because she knew the game. It upset her even more because it was increasingly happening in America, where people were supposed to be smarter and they were supposed to know better. The futility of her actions did not stop her, as her physical status was not of this scale. No one could see, feel or hear her, so her appeals had little effect on them. They had a great effect on me though. I knew that I could help her, because I really was here now, and what I did in this place could have effects. I knew she would know why I had returned, and that this would make her very pleased.

16

Emma was always questioning things. She had the ability to construct possible futures, not in some silly metaphysical sense, but because of her profound understanding and respect for deconstructing and rearranging the past into new more complex structures that could be tried and tested. Emma would ask questions just to throw thoughts out there. She knew if the questions didn't immediately develop answers, just thinking about the scope of each situation would eventually give rise to new models of describing them. And that in and of itself would help the situation immeasurably. The answer wasn't the hardest part of the question to figure out for her. The hardest part was re-describing the obviously incomplete existing descriptions for whatever events and relationships were being questioned. Once new models were achieved, just testing them out would cause answers to spill forth easily. Of course Emma also knew the state of 'science' when it came to human endeavors. She knew there was yet to be developed a more accurate 'physics' of complex human institutional/organizational arrangements. She knew the dangerous things that could happen as a result of supposedly 'scientific' information being applied to massive amounts of human beings and how they are organized. She had seen 'scientific management' used to extremes in Soviet Russia and Nazi Germany (and to a significant but less cruel extent in the United States – Taylor, its creator, was an American) and was disgusted by the new principles of organization supposedly scientific because they pursued an absolutely ordered industrial society.

"They never stopped to think that maybe order wasn't the best thing. They always just assumed that it was." Again I could see reflected in her remarks the knowledge that simplistic descriptions give rise to simplistic, and therefore abrasive (*violent*) behavior. *"They always thought*

that disorder was bad no matter what. Even when nonlinear physics proved otherwise!" Since her time ended not so long ago she had been more easily briefed on the advancements of earth up until the constantly expanding present. It had pissed her off even more so. *"Why is it that the book 1984 has been widely read for over 50 years now and yet the world still is the way it is without having rectified the authoritarian situations so clearly described within the book?"* I could feel her anger. I understood her pain. I tried to explain that although the book 1984 had done an immense favor for this world it left a feeling of great pessimism in most its readers by the time they finished it. It also supplied a concentrated manual for authoritarians to pick up and adapt new techniques. Not that more official manuals of this sort didn't already exist within many government bureaucracies. But it unknowingly offered totalitarian tactics (and an opinion that such events were inevitable and unavoidable) to a mass audience.

In fact *'plan B'*, as it was being called (*which should not be confused with lower level layers of the plan being called plan B - plan B was also the name of the overall plan, and that's what we've been referring to*), was exploiting loopholes left open within the book 1984. These authoritarians had constructed their scam well, avoiding any previous reference to the specific types of actions they were taking, to increase the probability of their plan working, without opposition because there was no specific precedent in method. For example, in 1984, it says:

> *"But by the fourth decade of the 20th century all the main currents of political thought were authoritarian. The earthly paradise had been discredited at exactly the moment when it became realizable. Every new political theory, by what ever name it called itself, led back to hierarchy and regimentation. And in the general hardening of outlook that set in round about 1930, practices which had been*

long abandoned, in some cases for hundreds of years --- imprisonment without trial, the use of war prisoners as slaves, public executions, torture to extract confessions, the use of hostages and the deportation of whole populations --- not only became common again, but were tolerated and even defended by people who considered themselves enlightened and progressive."

So the world's foremost authoritarians now use imprisonment without trial, but before a secret military tribunal. It's close enough to a trial, it would be argued. They use war prisoners not as slaves but as public relations pawns to better enhance support in their frightened publics. They execute people in secret, often in foreign countries where such practice is still allowed. They torture not to extract confessions, but to uncover terrorist plots. What concerned American would not be tricked into supporting torture of this type, when it would supposedly save lives? They use whole populations as hostages of the governments that are engaged in the conflict with each other. Authoritarians, despite their rigidity, have found ways of adapting. We must out-adapt them... and considering their rigidity, that shouldn't be as hard as one might think.

After I thought this Emma's smile even more enhanced my already existing optimism as a feedback response of her newfound optimism. We both knew that for the 1st time ever, those opposed to authoritarianism had the advantage. Better yet, we knew that people had finally realized that they had the advantage. That people had always had the advantage. We just never before realized it. Powerful institutions seem so big and strong and infinite in their ability. But they're not. They can be brought down nonviolently with only the right short set of words.

Emma directed me to a copy of an article from the September/October 2006 issue of Foreign Policy magazine. *"Read this. You'll need it."* She said. The article was called

'Empires with Expiration Dates.' I told her that I had already read it and I had come prepared with more information than this to stop what my return was intended to stop. The article quite nicely articulated that 20th century empires had become much shorter lived than empires of the past, but it thought this shrinkage was not permanent and could be 'fixed' so as to last long again. I told her that I had long ago figured out that actually, *it was* a permanently shrinking imperial time-span, and that they had missed this because it involved a nonlinear layering process of institutional growth that was currently unknown to people in the present. The only problem was that it was somewhat complex to understand. And this hypothesis needed to be able to be tested and understood by everyone, not just isolated intellectuals. This was the challenge.

17

It was said here that cockroaches would be the prominent species on earth after a nuclear holocaust. Is that what I meant when I said the meek shall inherit the earth? Maybe that's an extreme example. Many people had different interpretations of this passage about me in the bible, even though the word meek was quite clearly defined. And people had different interpretations about everything in the bible, even though most of them claimed to take its words literally. Believing that nonsense is truth was an everyday thing for them, so they missed out on a lot of information they came across. When you can see so many people, so far from objectively measurable reality, you can lose faith in the future of the species. Life becomes sad, constantly emotionally troubling.

Because cockroaches don't know much, they never developed skills of manipulation enough to screw each other over. Or maybe on their scale they do know something, and the scouts that risk their ass looking for food to bring back to the lair are the dumb-asses that got fooled by their cockroach leadership. I wasn't supposed to be the savior of the cockroaches. So this was not my concern. What was my concern was that people had become way too submissive because of this passage about the benefits of being meek. Even though I described no specific benefits. I only said that, somehow, they shall inherit the earth.

There are two definitions for meek. One is being submissive. The other is having humility and patience. Being humble and patient allows you to magnify power far beyond what it has so far achieved. It also helps to prevent you from concentrating too much power into the usual scenario where this concentrated power prevents further accelerated power from growing. Being submissive allows this horrible usual scenario to repetitively happen. Submissiveness prevents growth. It keeps you from attaining power. It makes power behave violently. Because when a system detects submissiveness, it responds with dominance. It automatically senses the opportunity. Promote your vulnerability, and you are begging to be attacked.

Power can be abused, and information is power. When power is abused, it prevents you from receiving more power, even though perceptual myopia most often times prevents people from noticing this. When people respond violently, it is most often the case that they feel powerless. At least relative to those who they behave violently towards. To solve this, give them more power. Respond to aggression by offering opportunities. Opening doors to better options close the doors to violent options. Satan was not amused. I don't think he agreed with my thoughts. We needed a demonstration of some sort. Something many people had thought about but not done before. This was not going to be that difficult in the middle of New York City. Especially today... There was an anti-war protest going on. People were everywhere. And there was always a volatile tension in concentrated populations. All you had to do was initiate a little funnel cloud amidst the concentrated quantity of people and it could magnify its growth well past handleable proportions. I didn't want to mess with anything that big right now, so I merely singled out someone that was very visibly pro-war. He was counter-protesting down the street and I thought he would work perfectly. I pretended like I knew him already and said, "How have you been?" "*Fuck off.*" He responded. I love New York. Next I said, "Come on, I just want to know what time it is." "*Don't you understand, hippie?*" People were so easily pushed over the edge emotionally when they thought they were superior to others. His face turned red and he prepared himself for violence, slugging me one in the stomach.

"Was that punch an accident?" I asked with a smile. The stranger replied, "*No. What are you, stupid?*" And then he hit me again. After confirming the intentionality of his actions, I responded with defensive maneuvers. I took out a $100 bill and offered it to him, saying, "Follow me into this office for much more than that." He took the bill and we walked into the office that this altercation had started in front of. Then I asked him, "What do you do for a living?" *"Options. Futures trading. Why?"* He was very perplexed by the way this situation had turned. I was sure Benjamin would be proud, and I could feel that I had brought his presence here for this. "Are you aware of which markets will adjust, and in which directions, should the increasing instability in the Middle East accelerate further?" *"Yeah. Why?"* "Are you aware of how to exploit inside knowledge ahead of time without revealing yourself through careless-ness?" *"Yeah. So?"* "Well, as fate would have it, the West intends to destabilize the Middle East into a multi-layered region-wide civil war. During and even more so *after* the region is very disorganized (*via this process*), Islamic fun-damentalists are being helped by the West to takeover most nationalist governments of the Middle East. Most of this reorganization will be completed by 2015. This includes at least Egypt, Saudi Arabia, Iraq, Pakistan and Lebanon. You've only yet seen Iraq. And although America will soon be attacking Iran, their government is already controlled by Islamic fundamentalists… so, while it will be attacked, the West will not take over that country… thanks to something you don't want me to tell you about. Have fun." He was stone cold silent. He wouldn't look at me. I continued, "What I am doing right now is not conditioning you to think that you will be rewarded by violence. I am showing you that you are being rewarded by talking to those you are opposed to rather than by being violent towards them. Do you understand?" When he did look at me, the look on his face was a frightened horror the likes of which I had not yet seen since I had returned. It was as if he had seen his future. "*Yes.*" He said shaking with what I detected was fear. And then he walked out of the office.

What I had told him was not necessarily true, and while I suspected he would doubt my claims, although he could feel the revelation of what I was saying, events themselves would soon change his mind from any doubt. Satan thought this was all very funny as we walked away down the street. "*I would've killed him. You are still such a pussy.*" He said. "My response was a well thought out multi-layered manipulation and you know that. Stop giving me shit." "*I know,*" he said laughing, "*you are learning very quickly.*" I knew many things about the greater complexity of the situation that had given me strategic advantages. Had he answered my very loaded questions differently, I would have answered very differently. But he had demonstrated himself to be like so many of the others. He was more than willing to profit off mass violence. His profession itself gave that away. His follow-up answers more than confirmed it. He had no idea the amount of money he was going to make. It was going to be a lot. And when his son was old enough to realize what his dad had done to make their family extraordinarily wealthy, twenty years from this very day… after knowing what had happened to this world since and how his father had been willing it to happen for the sake of money, like it was a football game he had bet on… his son not only took his own life, but before that he murdered their entire family. He murdered everyone, except for the father who had betrayed that family…

"*You are fucking ruthless.*" Satan was impressed. I was not. "I did nothing. He made his own choices. I merely supplied him with information, like nature does all the time. You know that too. You always use that shit on people. Throwing information out there that tempts." "*You know I don't! Information does that in every environment by itself. Consciousness perceives anything based on the information it is able to derive from its surroundings. I*

don't fucking exist. People make mistakes using informa-
tion and then feel guilty about it. They don't like that guilty
feeling so they pretend that something invisible tempted
them into doing it. To avoid responsibility and therefore,
damned to make the same mistakes again in the future. It is
the way they perceived the information they received that
made them do it. It is their own damn fault." "What I did
was dumb. Come with me." I dragged Satan around the
corner and down the street until we caught up with the man
I had given the information to. I called out to the man and
he came back over and sat with us talking on the corner for
another 30 minutes. I explained to him why it was not a
good idea to make money off the deaths of other human
beings and he agreed. I had this time changed his future for
the better. None of what I had said would happen to him
was going to happen to him. In fact now (*thanks to some
other things we told him*) he was going to make way more
money doing other things that resulted in no violence. After
this Satan and I walked down to a pizza place to get some
eats.

I told Satan, "Now my response to him is complete.
You thought I was done before." Satan snapped back, "*I
should've known you wouldn't accept ruthlessness as a
strategy.*" "I was trying to teach you a lesson too." I said
barking at him. "Revenge really is stupid. Particularly the
idiotic concept of magnifying your revenge when someone
harms you… This only causes more violent stupidity to
spill forth. Exemplified by my horrifying assessment of the
man's future… Accelerating violence does not prevent violence. This should be intuitively obvious to everyone. But
short-term profitable lies are powerful. People often get
tricked into serving power. You should know a lot about
that too." "*That I do.*" He said laughing. "*You've still got
such a hero-complex.*" I did feel kind of silly, like I was
Spiderman or something. I guess that was the sort of role I
was supposed to be playing here. People thought of gods

somewhat as superheroes. In the history of human litera-ture, heroes are often granted superhuman gifts by gods if they're not directly genetically related to gods. Even though this time, what I did can be done by anyone. No special powers necessary.

18

"*In the beginning there was the word. And with the word came the immediate knowledge that deception could be used against those who did not know words as well as you did. Thus began the still expanding network of lies throughout human history. If you're smart, you're expected to lie in order to exploit people. If you do not, you are dumb, because other smart people are out-exploiting you. In other words if you don't exploit people, what could be yours is being stolen by others who are willing to exploit people. If you don't exploit people, you are being exploited without responding back in kind.*" We're trapped into hurting people. There is no way to completely escape it. The institutions within our societies make us do harm, or they will punish us with more harm. It's a feedback process that uses our interconnectedness to make us compete ruthlessly against each other. And it works so well. So well in fact that most people are not even able to notice their part in it... Everything we buy, everywhere we work, nearly everything we do. All of our actions collectively are directed through this process. Success is not possible without other people failing. Or so people were conditioned to act. As if the methods by which interaction on earth took place were finalized and perfect. Methods that are described with language... Forceful language. Information could be very brutal indeed.

All information within the more technologically complex societies had been concentrated beyond what people thought was possible. New mathematics and logistical techniques had given the powerful leaders of those societies once again the means for increasingly totalitarian control over their publics. Every radio station, television network, newspaper, and magazine in America spouted the same lines when dealing with war. The promoters of war had set the initial conditions of what words were to be said, what frameworks those words were applied into, what concepts were the only necessary concepts to be paid attention to, usually distracting the public from any semblance of reality. And all within a relatively free press... They created the dynamical system of language that would be reflected throughout the entire period of the war. And this manipulation of perception would eventually lock in ever further when events based on these perceptions were caused. For instance, when the line about there being a clash of civilizations first began, the world was nowhere near remotely close to a significant separation and/or conflict between Islamic and Western cultures. These two entities were very diverse, very differentiated bodies of people that had just as many differences within themselves than they did with each other. All conversations continued however as if this was not the case. As if there was already a Muslim Caliphate running all the countries in the Middle East, and as if there was already a fully unified Western political body opposing it. The people promoting this line of thinking, of course, were trying to create these opposing political bodies by promoting them as already existing, and as the framework within which everyone should define/describe/associate events.

These promoters were very much in favor of the intentions of al-Qaida, and they intended to help al-Qaida bring them about. They were also in favor of this Western alliance. They were for the most part Westerners. So did people living in Western countries call these promoters of a clash of cultures traitors? No. Because these promoters spoke loudly, with authority, and because many of them worked inside the military bureaucracies of Western nations, they were perceived as heroes... or at worst as agitators, but definitely never as traitors. Even though these promoters' very clear and obvious goal was to help al-Qaida (*and any other Islamic fundamentalist group*) build its power so large that it controlled almost all of the Middle East. They knew at the same time that this building enemy would give them the public support for building their Western military bureaucracies up too, eventually aligning in an all-Western force. So because they were building themselves as well as their enemy, they were not perceived as traitors. They were totally growing the enemy however... al-Qaida would not have had a chance in hell of becoming as powerful as it would become without the help of America & its allies. The Western countries would make just the right public relations, logistical, and foreign policy mistakes to insure that al-Qaida grew as an enemy at an accelerated pace. I repeat again, because it is *so* important, that al-Qaida would have been a po-dunk backwoods fringe terrorist outfit, had it not been for Western help in building its organizational empire through this complex series of intentional mistakes. Most people in Western publics had no idea this was going on. People live their lives in their own overspecialized niches of activity, rarely having the time to pursue such intellectual adventures. So not only did they not know that al-Qaida was using us and being used by us to do this, but they did not know that in many other places this same sort of relationship was taking place. Iran is only another example.

Iran and al-Qaida are America's enemies, except that in reality they weren't. Iran, al-Qaida, and America were using each other to grow vast amounts of concentrated power for each other. They were in nonlinear alliances. Without each other effectively pretending to oppose each other (*although this involved real violence against each other*), none of them could build the structures of authority that all of them sought to build. These relationships were most often too complicated for their publics to understand and therefore stop for the additional reason that authoritarians inhibit education budgets in their nations. They know a slow and uninterested public is more likely to take shit. As in, they are easier to exploit.

"You will have to phrase it differently." I heard a voice say. *"Although what you said is fairly accurate, the meaning it conveys sounds conspiratorial. People have a hard time allowing themselves to understand something when it means some large conspiracy is going on. They don't like conspiracy. They have been conditioned to not believe it. And besides, conspiracy is not what's going on. It is the network of bureaucracies of all the world's countries that naturally repeats this beneficial authoritarian effect. Most in the world's military bureaucracies don't know they're helping their enemies. Just about all actually. And when they do realize it, they're caught in what they think is a catch-22. They cannot see how to avoid fighting and therefore (most often times) helping their enemies."*

Correct, sorry about that. Still, hundreds of thousands of people in almost every country must need this to keep happening. They worked for their military. And millions of others worked for companies affiliated with their country's military. It was their job. It was their career. That has even more identity attached to it. And the worst part about it was that they thought they were doing the noblest thing there is to do in their society. Try deprogramming that from all of a population. In many ways, they perceive that their life depends upon that process continuing. Although they never really consciously knew that this ***mutually beneficial authoritarian relationship between opposing countries*** was going on. Countries always just seemed to get into conflicts. Conflicts that are continuous, unending even. Diplomacy always seemed to fail. And yet bureaucracy: government and industry and religion, fed on this happening. Each country's collective bureaucracy ate the people that died in the conflict and grew bigger. This process of bureaucratic growth had never been adequately studied scientifically. So how could the problem ever be fixed?

Why has it not been studied enough to resolve the problem? It doesn't take a miracle to be able to see the process. And to test it with historical data.

It is usually thought that when countries fight each other, one invades the other and takes it over completely. It has won. Game over. One side wins, one side loses. The winner country's collective bureaucracy swallows the conquered and owns it all. And historically conflicts between countries happen this way a good proportion of the time. They also happen in other ways a good proportion of the time. Like the way I previously described.

Some time ago, a lot of people had jobs in the slave trade too. A lot of economic institutions relied on it continuing. The main sources of that were stopped. People found other jobs. Some people didn't want to. They were pissed. So everyone fought a war over it. What do they call that in substance abuse? Transference. We were going to need something to transfer the business of war to in a similar fashion. *"How about anything else?"* I heard the voice again. I could tell it was a woman's voice. I was sitting alone in a friend's office in Brooklyn. I ended up spending a lot more time talking to people that were still in the time-scale above the unfolding present than I did with people in the present. They were after all helping me do this. The woman that owned the voice came walking in through a wall. It was Eleanor. And she had brought a few friends.

19

"How in the hell do they get away with claiming something so ridiculous?!" Ayn was pissed. *"We really have a shitty memory when we're in the present. How could anyone forget the atrocities of all the communist dictators? This is a capitalist country for god's sake!"* I tried to explain to her that people didn't yet understand authoritarianism well enough as a science. So that label tended to float around on every country & political philosophy. Countries would use the label on each other all the time while never admitting to *being it* themselves... even though an authority accusing other countries of being authoritarian was itself an obvious authoritarian tactic, not enough people would notice. People didn't understand that the label '*authoritarian*' applied to every country, always. It was an actual measure of how much authority controlled their society, whether it be how they were allowed to dress &/or have sex with each other, or whether it was controlling the whole god damn economy.

People would hear of countries being totalitarian, communist, democratic, theocratic, fascist... a dictatorship, a republic... Some of the societal labels I just listed were even practically synonyms but hardly anyone could explain to you those distinctions. They just took those labels syntactically as totally different forms of government involving totally different things. They did not look at it (*or understand it*) as different levels of the same thing. Authority. *"But I didn't expect that capitalism would create the same kind of massive abuse of authority that communism did! Its inherent structure is supposed to prevent such occurrences!"* "Supposed to." I agreed. *"God damn it!"* Ayn yelled again. "Don't blame god, people damned it." I responded. *"It's a figure of speech. You know I don't give a damn about god."*

"*It's always perceived as necessary at the time.*" Eleanor interrupted. "*My husband did the same thing on a not so ruthless scale. But he still used authority to change the economic and social systems of the country at the time, to a more centralized government framework. An authority granted to him by a public devastated by a different authority that had pursued its own path of power concentration too far... That's the way it always seemed to take place. It was as if they were always doing it on purpose, except that, they weren't. Fate played a larger role in concocting complex event sequences than groups of men ever could. Humanity's own ignorance could always beat them at their own game.*" Ayn responded to Eleanor forcefully, "*Business? Is that what you're saying? Business as a whole in the country became too concentrated a power and that caused the economic system to fall apart?! Business caused its own leftist authoritarian response?*" "*Yes.*" Eleanor said quietly, with no arrogance. The kind of quiet in a voice that connotes a profound sadness... the spoken word of millions of lives that didn't need to be lost.

Ayn threw up. It wasn't like vomit didn't exist on the more complex time scale. Intense human emotion still existed too, even more so. And such devastating information that Ayn knew (*minds check empirical validity quickly there*) was all too accurate overwhelmed her system. Understanding horror is a painful but necessary task. Suddenly the door to the room opened, as if the preceding sequence had been already foreseen and planned for, and Ernesto came in with a towel and something to drink for Ayn. Ernesto tried to comfort her, "*You know, we all fucked up, it's ok once you realize how the world will change for the better... if they realize it, that is... it's already too late for us. You've got to tell them this, Jesus.*" "I know." I said nervously. "And please stop calling me Jesus. That's a little too much pressure, don't you think, you guys aren't really making it easy on me." "*Life isn't supposed to be easy,*"

90

Eleanor came back into the conversation, "*It is people trying to force life into systems that make it more simple than it is, that end up causing it to be more difficult than it would otherwise be. Simplicity causes a more dangerous complexity to emerge because the existing complexity is ignored.*"

Ayn drank some more water, shrugged and said, "*I guess we're going to have to watch and see how it ends up turning out. Hoping that individuals eventually understand enough to stop this feedback loop from continuing.*" Ernesto jumped in, "*Hope should have very little to do with it. Individuals will act, and the complexity with which they act will determine the adaptability of the human species. If Jesus and others succeed in their missions, people should be well on their way to adapting more fluidly. It's hard to believe that I, of all people, can't wait to see a capitalist system develop that succeeds in preventing its inherent concentration of power tendency from occurring, without any need of a concentrating government power to prevent that tendency. Business has a long way to go before it gets there legitimately.*" "I've already written an economic paper that lays this out." I said. "I'm not sure how it will be received in the current geopolitical climate though." "*All you have to do is get people to conduct the experiments that test it, and it will be handled.*" Ayn and Eleanor said at the same time.

"*You do that by getting the idea out there in every way that you can.*" Ernesto asserted. "*I've been a leader of a successful leftist (socialist) authoritarian organization. I know that both capitalism and socialism can be used by authoritarians to concentrate government power & institutional power in general – they concentrate and expand authority [tyranny] – democracies can dissipate & therefore lessen any concentrations of authority [liberty]. Capitalism & socialism are very similar in certain ways because they are opposites. These 2 opposites are more dynamic ver-*

sions of the tyrannies that had always existed before in human history. So they were less tyrannical at first, but given the opportunity (which each consistently had & perpetually will have), they could produce massively destructive, highly ordered tyrannies like the world has never before seen. Fascism in Germany and subsequently everywhere else that newer more complex levels of business-friendly totalitarian government spawned on earth was the result of the concentration of industrial power. Communism in Russia and subsequently everywhere else that newer more complex levels of anti-business totalitarian government spawned on earth was the result of the concentration of government power to counteract concentrations of industrial power. Free thinking people in democracies are the best chance to stop this increasingly destructive feedback loop between these conflicting economic systems."

"*Agreed.*" Benjamin said with a big smile as he nonchalantly walked through the door. He was back. And we were all very happy to see him. "*I think I've found some ways to begin this process of economic and political transformation.*" He said, making us all excited to see what he had come up with. "*They think capitalism has already won that battle. They're wrong. As if you can win a feedback loop, hah. Win how, by stopping it from continuing to move back and forth? That's suicide! They've even moved on to new enemies as if they're right. But they cannot escape the internal flaws that exist within their too-simple capitalism.*"

20

"Since I've been 'trapped', so to speak, on the scale above the present, I've had the time to work on much more complex models for the present to implement. Where my colleagues and I at the time had left off in America before, I have continued for at least another hundred years past the current present. These things move ever faster, you know. So my description you receive now will possibly not even last that long. The exponential curve is getting very steep, hah. Don't ever forget this. But also don't ever retreat to a crudely simplistic format that abandons all thus far developed complexity. That is what usually occurs when a society suffers significant loss of function or death (when it cannot outpace the increasingly complex environment), so if a society barely survives under a too-simplistic format, I consider it dead, for if it is not clear that it is already in an intense state of decay, soon enough (at its point of criticality) its cataclysmic depressurized dissipation will leave no doubt." Benjamin knew his shit. That guy should have lived longer than eighty-four years.

*"It will be hard for them to see how capitalism is **not complex enough** in the current time, for they see it to be incredibly complex, as complex as it has ever been, so much so that most people on earth hardly even understand how it works. This is true of course. But we're dealing with an accelerated curve, so we'll always be at the point where we are more complex than we've ever been. Unless we mess up and end up having to recover from catastrophes... And we can only mess it up when most people do not understand what is going on (when they aren't allowed to be a real part of it)."*

"Capitalism today has reached the stage where it openly causes mistakes in order to exploit them. Intentional instability they sometimes call it." I said to Benjamin. *"Ahh the predetermined mistake of trying to bank off intentionally making mistakes. They are close to getting past this stage just by reaching it. I hope the current tendency doesn't hold."* "What do you mean?" I asked. *"In the present, where you are now, organizations usually try to milk a technique until it runs dry. Similar to how they exploit resources. If they do that with this stage of intentional instability there will be great destruction before the next stage is reached, even though it is easy to reach. And even though capitalism will be way more profitable when it is reached, when intentionally causing chaos is tactically abandoned."*

This intentional instability stage of Capitalism occurred after it defeated Socialism in their epic battle, I thought. *"There was never really a battle there. It was ignorant people just getting into conflict by relying on oversimplistic descriptions. Not the first time that's happened, hah."* Now I could see what he meant. Capitalism and Socialism could have been studied together. The battle between them did not need to happen. Let alone a battle that could have resulted in the nuclear annihilation of nearly the entire human population. There must have been other reasons that people did that. There had to be other reasons deemed beneficial so that people would want to make that battle happen. Economic theory debate sessions did not tend to produce such violence at schools. Most people thought it was boring. But in this, not only did people care, but they nearly destroyed the world asserting their opinion. And that's what it was. Opinion. Economics is supposed to be a science, but it has a long way to go before it earns the peer-reviewed respect of say, biology, and most of my followers didn't even believe biology was real. Indoctrination is a harder thing to deal with after the fact.

Benjamin was not interested in which political or economic ideology/philosophy won, nor which winning persons would put those thoughts into action. He had been thinking long enough to recognize what winning really was. *"If this is to be successful for any length of time there must be eternal vigilance. There must be the knowledge by all that change of order must constantly continue or it will be imposed upon you by nature."* He erupted, *"Life would no longer go on as it had always gone on---that is, badly."* As Benjamin continued to speak, he seemed to be the incarnation of a great many minds relaying information all at once. *"Life is a multi-layered mixture of interacting dynamical systems. If all of these are not given their necessary accelerated increase in freedom, life will no longer go on here. The interconnecting networks of dynamical systems will return to a more static, simple state of little if any autonomous motion. Humanity's power is past the point of greatness that can bring this about in an instant... if humanity cannot constantly change its political and economic ordered structures toward greater complexity & fluidity fast enough, complex life here will end."*

Benjamin knew that life did not always go on badly, but that life for most of humanity *had* been so, since its development into societies, because of the repressive ordered systems implemented by simple, controlling minds. Life in general (*including all species*) always began crudely and violently, because it needs time to develop into more complex/fluid forms that can eventually achieve a co-existence with the totality of life by increasingly minimizing abrasive violent interactions. The initial sets of species in evolution were of course the most abrasive because they had the least information gained from existing in time. Life had up to this point just emerged within time, so how could it already have mastered this? It needs millions of generations one after the other, learning and adapting to the changing environments of time, before it could even recognize itself enough to do this to such an extent that it did not physically destroy the space with that which it came into contact with. Particularly other forms of life it came into contact with.

Ernesto jumped in after hearing my thoughts, *"Actually, this initial brutality helped create the initial structures of life. Feeding on the destruction of one another."* "I know." I said. "That's why everything starts out crappy, and yet, that early version provides a foundation from which to build better. Complex enough life learns to increasingly feed on things that are dynamically further away from itself." *"Nicely done."* Eleanor said softly in my ear as she walked by. Ayn still looked pissed, although she was feeling better.

Benjamin then stated what he considered to be a necessary presupposition of the structure of matter in motion itself. *"Whenever conflict occurs it is a clear indication that more mixing must occur. Difference of opinion can be rectified with clever combination of positions. Real mixes of positions, not a partisan fraud, because nature succumbs to no ruse."*

21

It really was just like any organization. About a thousand people regularly go to the organization's building. Each of them giving a little money to the organization during the visit… and as a whole the organization earns thousands of dollars per week. The organization uses this money to build more buildings and pay the organization's owners and labor. The organization's owners get progressively more and more wealthy, and the organization's territory expands.

"An organized religion is an institution. It is a hierarchical organization. It is a bureaucracy. It is many different people working in different positions to grow that organization. That is every organization's primary goal. To expand itself… forever. A religious organization is only using a religion as its catalyst to expand. It does not care about the religion. The religion is just a tool for it to gain authority and expand the organization's power. The power it gets is totally dependent on how powerful the catalyst is at convincing more and more people to expand the organization. So the religion must convince people to build this bureaucracy. What is preached as the religion must increasingly become better at convincing people to give more of their time and energy in pursuit of the organization's growth. This growth/expansion comes from the organization tying itself to religious and political and economic causes. Religious and political and economic causes are the ultimate appeal to people's motivations. To intensify people's psychological (and actual) need for those religious and political and economic causes, the religion must create conflict. When violence increases, people become more afraid. They are more vulnerable to being convinced into building the bureaucracy of their religion (which, as previously stated, is only to build the bureaucracy, the re-

ligion is only the manipulative tool used to grow that or-ganization). Violence works. If you want to get power, de-stabilize situations. Create conflict. Then rally people to your side. You just have to cause the violence. Once people have been inflicted with violence they will increase the vio-lence from there for you, like little chaotic self-organizing pawns. All you need to do is create the initial momentum."

Anyone who ever willingly tried to do this sort of thing would probably be classified as clinically psychotic nowadays, I thought. The techniques must be known in or-der to prevent them from working, not so that more people can use them. The difficulty is the natural gray area that exists everywhere. I don't ignore it. I deal with it. Using the dynamics of creating instability is incredibly valuable. But, like all things, the crudest, easiest and most immediate value to extract is that which is extracted through violence. This of course is far from the most valuable dynamics, which are extracted from carefully skilled techniques that prevent violence from being mathematically possible. Fluid dynamics was the most complex... they were the most valuable. In other words, instabilities increased their value when their use tended towards less violence in extracting that value. The more fluid their behavior was...

22

Satan was always hilariously arrogant. He just kept going, and I was laughing too hard to ask him to stop. *"Look at me! I'm responsible! Blame me! Conceal yourself! I will take the blame for all your sins, so you never have to correct your behavior! Just keep tossing the bad things you do in my court. Shit... Keep thinking you're doing anything wrong! Then throw that wrong at me. I'll make it go away so you keep repeating the behavior. You must like what you're doing! Or you wouldn't go to such great lengths to hide it. I'll keep hiding it for you. All you have to do is keep blaming me. You'll never change. And I'll still never exist. But you'll never be accountable for anything! Blame me, and you get away with whatever you want!"*

We both started crying we were laughing so hard. Then we were just crying. Then we started laughing again. It really was very sad. And it really was very funny too. Were we supposed to deny our feelings? Even when they conflict? There is value and understanding in the full range of the feeling. Ignorance is usually funny and sad. Accountability, and what happens when masses of people dodge it, was something that was still little understood by the human population. Probably because they had prevented themselves from seeing it in order to not be looked down upon by laughing at it, or probably for some other reason. He wasn't done amusing himself, *"It wasn't the devil... **the humans did it to themselves!** But they couldn't accept or understand that... so I'll persist as their punching bag. I'll be part of the TV show they're pretending is their real life."*

They certainly have a hard time, I thought. People always seemed to get in the same sort of trouble. Over and over again... Satan wasn't too subtle about it. He actually seemed really pissed, which is not out of character for him. I guess a being would get sick of being blamed all the time for things he knew he didn't do. Especially when he knew he didn't even exist. With newfound brilliance and a seemingly novel assurance of his reality, Satan took in a breath and grew big-chested with the pride of a conquering animal. *"I know all. I am needed. Therefore I will pretend to exist."* I guess even mythology needs a little identity uplift every once in a while. Sometimes that uplift went overboard. I could sense it coming. He was about to spit fire. I couldn't even finish describing my pre-awareness of the words he was about to use before Satan interjected, *"They can't hide their violence from me! I'm the devil! I know every act of violence that has ever happened or ever will happen. I know that some of the leaders of terrorist organizations, primarily al-Qaida and Hezbollah, are well aware of the beneficial relationship that exists between them and Western bureaucracies. These particularly clever leaders are well aware of how enemies feed off each other. Of course there are Western leaders that are also aware of this relationship. It is the horrifyingly hilarious tendency of military organizations no matter what their size. You'll have to explain this relationship to everyone, because even some of the leaders on both sides have no idea that this is going on."*

Accept responsibility. It was something they could never do. They could not hold themselves accountable for their own actions, or else very bad thoughts would weigh on them. Inconceivable amounts of pressure constantly threatened them back into denying their own role in life. "It couldn't be that simple," they said, constantly lying to themselves. The world can be a big and scary place, if you ignore it for years. To turn back at any progressively further point, becomes increasingly mentally devastating. No one person's psychology can handle failing on that massive a scale. With this picture you can see the entire chain of human cowardice throughout history build up an incredible amount of responsibility that it merely left drifting unresolved in its wake. You can also see the reinforcing nature of this repeated behavior. The cowardice took on a life of it's own after a certain point. Any behavior will. You just need to start it in its initial direction. I understand the pressure everyone unknowingly gets into. They're largely brought up in it. Once you're smart enough in life to realize it you've already racked up too much to deal with.

I told Satan that fate played a larger role than he was giving it credit in these things he was yelling about. *"Yes, fate being that which remains left for human beings to manipulate. If they don't realize what they're doing now through long entrenched deterministic processes, they will soon. After they hear from us, hah. So then, all that did not know will know. And they will try."* I reminded Satan that it would not be a good idea to try to enhance these beneficial authoritarian relationships between enemies at the expense of the citizens of all countries. I reminded him that humans must get past this stage of political disaster. Or they will knock themselves backwards a few hundred years. *"That's their record so far."* He was right. But his pessimism pissed me off.

"You know how many people on earth still argue that authoritarian government is a great way to run a country? So damn many! It's amazing they can even tie their shoes they're so stupid." "Apparently there's something keeping them trapped in such stupidity. People would not accept such obviously faulty conclusions unless they had been coerced in some manner." *"Guess who?"* The way he said it told me he knew exactly whom or what coerced people. *"I'll give you a hint. You've been looking for him. And here's another hint. It's not a person. It's a physical representation of power. The so called legitimate means by which power is exerted in human affairs."* Let me think. *"It's authority!"* He didn't care about me discovering it for

myself. "*They're all afraid of themselves. Their own authority keeps them locked in. All authority is a constant reflection back at everyone involved in upholding it of why they should be afraid. And so, why they should continue that authority; they accidentally reinforce their own fears. Their fears of each other... Their fear of change.*"

I wasn't quite sure what to make of what Satan was saying. Now he wasn't really making sense to me. "*It is their mistaken obsession with rationality; with order; and with absolute descriptions. They so think they're right all the time. They're not right! They're not even close and they have no idea that they'll never be close! The further time goes, the further away they'll become! And they'll never even realize that that's the beneficial way toward growth! They'll think further away is negative.*" Now I got it. "They won't always think that." I told his pompous ass. He wasn't so sure. "*They are nowhere near close enough to understanding real freedom yet. They're still too busy using the word freedom as a rhetorical trick for authoritarianism.*" He did have a point. But he was being negative to make his point.

"*We both know which countries will be the major world powers of the twenty-first century, right?*" "Yeah, so?" I said. "*Well, three out of five of them are currently authoritarian, and the other two are moving towards authoritarian models to better compete with the other three! Instead of the other way around!*" Again, he had a point. I would've gotten pissed again, but I saw how his point could be used to reverse the tendency his words were revealing. He must have seen this too. "*You still doubt my ability? Hah, funny.*" On most occasions, not just when hanging around this guy, I wasn't the only arrogant asshole in the room.

"*Here's another hint.*" He said. "*Mixing. The science of mixing is everything.*" I get it. Iran & the US are getting into conflict with each other. This means they are currently attracted towards each other and they will mix. They are mixing violently rather than fluidly because both sides chose conflict and the 'confrontational approach'. They did not choose to cooperate. One way or another, they are going to mix together. This is going to happen. Elements of each society's structure will emerge/meld within the other. How they mix determines the structure their mixing will create. Via war: autocracy - Via cooperation: democracy. In Iran this means: an *even more* authoritarian system, an even more religious fundamentalist political party run theocratic structure than they already are. In the US this means: a *more* authoritarian system, in a more religious fundamentalist political party run theocratic structure.

Both societies could be cooperatively mixed into a much less authoritarian structure, each developing much more of a multiple-party democracy, consistently changing with little or no institutional religious influence. But their current actions suggest they don't want that. Their current actions suggest they desire towards total control. And unbeknownst to them all, this meant they desired total failure. Every nation seemed to. China was soon going to be the latest dominant world economic power on earth. And they were painfully authoritarian. Their economic power came primarily in numbers of humans. There was very little innovation inside authoritarian structures. That which had a momentum of *not* changing built up the longest, was the hardest to change. This sort of doomed inertia was the only trajectory leading by example. And since its doom was not immediate, it was taken to be a good example.

The same slothful behavior was happening not only with China and countries that wanted to be more like it, it was happening to companies too. Innovation always seemed to slow as power grew. Satan went off, "*You think the oil industry is going to innovate alternative energy sources? Hah! You think the auto industry is going to create safer and more fuel-efficient cars? They're the last enti-*

ties that would do such a thing! Each these examples are the slowest because they are still banking on the old source of profit. The fastest and the strongest will always be someone new! We must never rely on the old power to change itself! A new power must always emerge with a new idea that replaces the old. We must dissipate the old power so that new people have their chances." "Easier said than done." I told him. *"Not so! Easier done than said!"* I thought how. *"Size is not everything! The most powerful institutions on earth seem very omnipotent, but they're the most impotent! The bigger & more concentrated they are, the slower they are."*

I got distracted. Too much information... Too many ideas... My understanding was slowing with the wind. It seemed like it was there as much as the wind was there. This was the first time I noticed that thought was a part of fate.

23

"Power is such a complex process. How are think-ing beings ever supposed to live with it, when every time you learn more you become able to abuse more?" The complexity wasn't lost on me. But as I walked around many cities in the world, one of the most prevalent states of mind among people was that they were not even thinking about this. They were all locked into serving power. Some particular power, that is. They all were serving the interests of different bureaucracies. Wherever by chance they happened to live, they toiled to grow the beast. And they were happy to do it. It was very sad to see. And it was everywhere. Didn't matter what country... and there wasn't a psychological identity mechanism that wasn't being used to do it. Literally, every action of every person in some way benefited the growth of some organization. Some more than others... But this same process had been done over and over again over nearly every inch of the earth. This same rigid, decaying, self-destructive institutional lock-in was coating the surface of the earth like a living organism. And it wasn't a living organism. It was supposed to be a helpful aid to a living organism. Something to help us organize things... Something to help us...

This expansion of power in societies usually grew larger until the society encompassed more territory. It invaded and took over other societies if it was powerful enough to do so. Any country that got remotely powerful in its own area tried to do this. Power + Territory = Country. How's that for a hilariously over-simplistic description? The definition of empire is debated, however. Rightfully so... But it usually refers to when this process of a certain country's power & territory expansion reaches a significant area. It is effectively a natural competitive growth process. When some country's reign extends spatially and lasts for a long enough time it is considered an empire. *"Exactly how long is long enough... is not necessarily important."* Benjamin had guided me to my hypothesis of empires. He had told me to write about it so that others could test it and if proven empirically accurate, national behaviors could be modified to prevent the inevitable disasters the hypothesis predicted would come.

As time went on, the empires that each future generation built extended further, with more control over a larger amount of territory than its predecessors. It was obvious that simple-minded people would then assume that the world itself could eventually be taken. That eventually, an empire would come about on earth that successfully took total control over earth. This of course was not going to be the case, but the powerful people of today's world didn't know that. And like all their predecessors, they wanted to be that empire. They were at least going to try. *"Bad luck."* Satan said. *"I laugh every time they try. But this time I'm laughing harder than I ever have. Because we get to stop them from ever trying again."* Funny, I thought. *"Go ahead. Tell them about the compression."* "All in good time." He was going to spoil it. "I guess now's as good a time as any." I buckled too easily.

As time went forward, the length of time *it took* the world's empires *to expand* their territorial & economic control was lessened. It took the Roman Empire hundreds of years to control what the Nazis took in five years. There were many, many examples of this. The opposite was also experimentally verifiable. The length of time each of the world's empires *held* their territorial & economic control lessened. The Roman Empire roughly held its control over its territory for hundreds if not over a thousand years. The Nazis held their territory for about five years. Then came the really interesting part. This lessening was an accelerated curve. So as we go into the future, the length of time it takes to occupy *and lose* control over territory (and its economic assets) gets compressed ever faster until there is no more time to do either.

We in the present time are rapidly approaching that point in time where no time is allotted for taking or losing control of land & its value. The world's nations do not know this yet, so they still try. Until now.

There is also the degree of autocracy each empire holds in its society's structure that plays a role. The more autocratic an empire's internal structure is, the quicker that empire fails, dissipating the authority abruptly and violently, because those in charge of it chose the more autocratic structure. Some experimental evidence for this: Nazi empire's time-span: 12 years. Soviet empire's time-span: 70 years. US empire's time-span so far: 230 years. The United States is much less autocratic than the Soviets were, and the Soviets, while very autocratic, were less so than the Nazis. But the United States is currently moving toward an increasingly autocratic structure at an accelerated pace. Benjamin always used to tell us, *"Whenever you give up freedom, security goes down."* He would constantly warn us that whenever someone advised trading freedom for security, whether they knew it or not, they were helping a tyrant. There is no currently existing societal empire older than the United States. They were all too autocratic and have therefore died. If the United States is not careful, it will kill itself. It is only still around today because of the significant bit of democracy it has made reality in its short history.

No matter how autocratic or democratic you are... the compression still takes place ever faster. This is an emergent occurrence of the increasingly interdependent & complex institutional network of bureaucracies worldwide. Autocracy just speeds up the decay process even more. The United States *could* reverse its imperial course. That article had stated (amongst other things) an incomplete obvious... that an empire must gain more through its conquests than it costs to conquer, or it will not try. This calculation is dangerously oversimplified for what certain decisions based on it will cause. Powerful people had yet to understand the many ways in which there was an immense amount more to gain by not trying. The profit of allowing for more complex individualistic institutional layers to emerge was unknown to them.

This universe is a game of numbers. Benjamin had said, *"America must divide and subdivide its institutions of power indefinitely into the future, instead of trying to divide and conquer others. As fast as it can...Where now there are three supposedly equally opposing branches of government, in the future, if it is to survive, there will be four, then five, then ten, eventually as many as thirty and more. This is the nature of the dissipation of authority. Power must always be balanced and checked with increasing complexity or it bursts. One must not fight this inevitability. Those that seek advantage must seek to create and expand not merely by concentration, but also by dissipation of power."*

24

Power was always concentrating. This concentration effect was an actual physical force of nature that had not yet been discovered. Oh it was described to a limited extent in a few scientific disciplines, but not in the particular capacities and scope that it operated in within society. Science had too difficult a time objectively studying something so subjective. And authority was all too often not interested in letting science tell it what to do. How it should work. That it should change. This turned a very difficult challenge into a near insurmountable challenge. But things would not always be this way. Unbeknownst to most authorities, science was increasingly having an effect over how authority was structured and what it was permitted to do. This increasing role that science played was on an accelerated curve. And I couldn't wait to see the look on authority's face when that exponential curve got close to vertical.

Authority's actions and legitimacy were fading at an accelerated pace, and surely those bureaucracies of authority would resist their inevitable demise. Once the science got to a very interesting and critical point however, authority itself would gladly deconstruct into more fluid forms. That critical time is near. The holdup seemed to be that authorities did not really know how to increasingly create more fluid institutional layers within societies. *"All they had to do was look at how they had already historically done it."* Benjamin's voice echoed through the halls of the building I was in. *"Split power up and its divided parts have more room to grow. Physically check it with balances constantly. This is usually forced from outside, but if they became willing, authorities shall expand infinitely as they deconstruct themselves into smaller more agile components. This is part of dissipating it."*

Power was also always dissipating, Benjamin had said. This dissipation effect was the same physical force as the concentrating effect, merely the opposite side of the force. There was no positive or negative to these opposing sides... without both concentration and dissipation occurring increasingly quicker, any society that existed would decay until it was no more. *"I call this force part of the same force that biologists call evolution and physicists call entropy. Part of the force others generally call time."* Benjamin's echoes bounced off the walls. *"Society is breathing."* He had told me that without bouncing back and forth between these two opposing states at an increasingly fast speed, societies self-destruct. They decay. He said that this process has always gone on in societies. Before they knew of their existence, or, before people had sufficiently described the force, those that accidentally bounced ever quicker between concentrating and dissipating power were the so called fittest. I say fittest only in the sense that those societies that did this better than others, lasted longer. And how this was done got intricately more complex with many emerging layers as time went on.

America's most powerful people seemingly objected to the proven idea of dissipating authority. I think the idea itself even emerged in America. But as usual, the managers weren't the scientists. Consolidation was the goal of the managers. So the war on terrorism was constructed to meet these consolidation ends. Authority was going to toss the biggest pile of bullshit ever at its public. This is always what authorities did of course, but as time progresses the pile becomes increasingly massive. This would be the biggest pile ever. However, I had the feeling that people had lost their preference for the taste of bullshit. Many Americans thought the terrorist threat was overblown. And it was. But they neglected to see a lot of behind the scenes right-wing authoritarian actions. They neglected to see the self-interest that some people had in growing the terrorist threat.

American authoritarians want there to be an apocalyptic threat. They want it so badly, that they are actually trying to influence it to happen.

Many people here in America are so into 'end times' prophecy. I noticed it everywhere. Culturally, the promotion of 'end times' had been a giant victory for religious fundamentalists. But most people interested in it were the undereducated manipulation victims. Those most susceptible to authoritarian influence... Everyday on TV, whole channels would spout off crap quoting the bible and manipulating people into taking sides on whether or not the end of the world was real. Every detail of the Book of Revelation, (which was honestly all my fault), was constantly discussed. And it all circulated around a few particular story elements. As often times perceptions do. Everybody had an opinion on them. Usually an unsubstantiated opinion, it makes the shows more entertaining that way. Of course I knew what was really happening, so I had to jump in this stupid game. I saw the most paranoid thoughts attracting themselves toward one story element: the mark of the beast. It was so obvious to me. Probably because I already knew what it was. Yet it was so far away from everyone else. The mark was clearly visible to everyone that was speculating absurd notions about it. And they still couldn't see it. They even had the best damn clue in that stupid book to help them figure it out. And they still overreached it. And therefore missed it completely. I knew how badly they wanted to find it too, so they could parade around proclaiming even more fake proof that the end really was about to come. I knew that when I revealed it, as a historically interesting coincidence, it would not be taken in that light. It would be a profound & disturbing exposure of the hell they had no idea was already amidst them. It would shock them horribly. But that's what they were being conditioned to want.

My revealing of this was to help deprogram them, not to make them even more zealous. But that decision was not entirely in my hands. They had to realize on their own that any culture is so big and complex that it accidentally (and therefore coincidentally) manifests its thoughts and ideas throughout the language inherent in its complex systems. So if a culture has myths associated with certain things, by chance those things will appear at times within its political and economic circumstances. Not that it gives legitimacy to the myth, although this is what people usually thought, but because society reflects back the ideas and language that helped create it. The mark of the beast, as they had dutifully memorized it, was 666. The scripture said quite clearly that you cannot buy or sell without the number of the beast. And yet because of the mental clouding of zealotry (*which produced all sorts of ridiculously absurd theories*), all the interpretations of these descriptive passages were far from recognizing the mark for what it was. What mark is necessary to buy and sell? What mark can you not do without in the process of business & exchange? There is only one mark that fits the description with the utmost clarity. This mark is involved in every transaction of business on the planet. Without this mark, transaction cannot take place. Is it obvious what this mark is yet? What information do you need in order to buy or sell all products and services? I knew he wanted to say it, so I opened the floor to my partner to describe it, because it probably should be this way.

"*Thank you Jesus.*" Satan said with the biggest smile I'd seen him smile yet. "Stop calling me Jesus. I'm not Jesus." And then he said it. "*The mark... is price.*" "But which price?" I asked even though I knew. This was one of the big moments he was most excited about, so I had to give him his day. "*The most common price of course, in the most common currency!*" "Why would any particular price be the most common price?" I asked again knowing full

112

well the answer to my question. Satan responded again to my prompt as if he was a loyal pet. *"Because of marketing deception!"* "There's a lot of marketing deception involved in economic systems, which deception do you speak of?" He was laughing and drooling so profusely when he spoke as if this brought very good memories to him. *"The very first deception of course! The foundation of deception in any economy based on numbers! Which are all economies, hah. Numbers have multiple digits. But you can remove a digit in a number by making it a miniscule amount less in price! The psychological effect of this one less digit deception occurs in all cases of buying and selling using numbers! It's even a deception that's so old and obvious that most people don't fall for it consciously, although they still may sometimes subconsciously. But it still deceives all new people in the market, each new generation. It is still the simplest trick, the very foundation of all deception involving money. It occurs in many prices, in every base of 10, but it occurs most frequently in one particular place. And it continues everywhere, to this day."* "Keep going!" I egged him on. He was so enjoying this. *"The mark of the beast is $9.99!"* Nobody ever noticed it. Even though they only had to turn it upside down to see.

"The mark is almost always there even when it's not exactly that price! Even when it subtracts a number and not a whole digit... $59.99, $179.99, $8999.99 - it is the foundational deception pattern from which all price follows. For some reason, nobody ever dares to sell a product for $10.00! That's four digits! When it could be perceived as three digits in people's minds! It's not sixty dollars! It's fifty-something dollars!" The whole thing was very funny. Because it demonstrated how readily we all become followers, particularly when we see an advantage, no matter how small. *"That's the way it's always worked!"* Adam yelled as he walked up to us, slapping Satan a high five as he walked by him. He was eating an apple too... everyone

in the time scale above the present got a kick out of making fun of the ludicrous stories the present had developed. Adam continued, *"That's how I came up with my best work. Everyone independently following their own advantage, their self-interest, freely. I remember noticing these little dynamical quirks throughout every economic system I studied, and finally it came to me. There is an order here, but it is a free order. An order directed only by everybody's combined independent inclinations."* This was the first time I thought that I knew how totalitarian governments could develop easily from democracies, and vice versa. No one could see Satan or Adam, so I communicated my side of the conversation with thoughts. Adam seemed to be ignoring my thoughts; he just kept on talking. And I was happy he did.

"Economics really would be a dismal science, if it were a science at all. Those douche-bags took my testable theory and assumed all sorts of bullshit on top of it. I guess self-interest prefers short-term profit, even over science." He was quite pissed. *"I bitched about monopoly in my most famous book. Nobody remembers that part. Of course I bitched about monopoly in an 18th century framework, so why would they? But it still applied, damn it!"* Then he turned to me as if what he was saying additionally implied that somehow I was at fault. *"You think Christianity was stupid when it dissipated its authority throughout Europe and beyond into Protestantism? Zealotry (the tendency to try to get as close as one can to absolutely concentrating power) gains a little, dissipation gains so much more. Christianity would not have successfully expanded nearly as far as it did had it not allowed itself to split into ever-greater numbers of competing organizations. You can be damn sure that the Popes through this period didn't want this to happen. They wanted the Catholic Church to continue to control it all. But this monopolistic tendency is something to resist."* He talked himself up into a greater

114

and greater emotional episode. *"Right now, the largest companies in the US are more powerful than almost every country on earth. Soon, even medium sized companies will be way more powerful than the strongest governments in the world. All previous governmentally based threats will be piss-ants. There will no longer be security threats from them. And this will be without these companies being affiliated in any way with defense or security applications. In fact, their self-removal from these industries of war will be necessary to achieve this corporate growth. If they do, the accelerated technological expansion itself will give them more than enough **knowledge** to deter violence, without any necessity of developing defense systems. Then even relatively small companies will outpace the power of the most powerful governments. And as this is all happening, new and even more individualistic institutional layers can emerge that generate even more magnifications of profit. Why don't we just... get to speeding this process up already?"*

25

I couldn't believe I was seeing all these guys sitting at the same table. The thought of it was beyond impossible to any human that was knowledgeable of their opposing historical accomplishments. I still had a hard time believing it, except for the fact that I was used to how things operated on the time-scale above the unfolding present. There was more intentional mixing of ideas there. They had none of the usual intense disrespect for each other as humans of such widely differing conclusions have on earth in the present. If your conclusions or hypotheses or opinions were different there, they would seek each other out for constructive combination. No particular person amongst them would at all try to monopolize the debate or in any way weight the argument in their favor. They would literally attempt, as best they all could, to combine their ideas equally and test the complex combinations they came up with, with experiments. Deception was not necessary in this scenario because winning was much more understood by them than by people in the beginning of the twenty-first century. Winning was not confined to 1 specific competition, nor was losing the horribly paralyzing negative of the form it had appeared in human history thus far. This was a result of the more complex understanding of opposites. It was a result of their more complex understanding and knowledge of everything they had dealt with, which was beyond the scope of humanity's experience... until now. When there was an attempt to outpace one of the others in these theoretical & experimental sessions, it was to outpace each other in achieving a combination that represented a more equal combination of each other's values and properties of ideas than each other's descriptions had achieved before. It was realized that the more detailed the mixing was that went on between them (*the more they mixed their different ideas equally in ever more infinitely complex pro-portions*), the more development that would occur. If some-thing was left out or not sufficiently represented in the mix, they would not have as complex a combination as they could have, and this would be to their detriment.

"When the world's interaction in the present be-comes like these men behave," Satan said, *"there will be no need for me anymore. And I will go away happily."* "If only non-living bureaucracies of authority were as willing to disband themselves as you are." I said to him. *"Someday."* He said laughing. We were both still watching these men on the more complex time-scale solving problems of such inordinate complexity that it would make anyone in the present literally lose their mind. Karl was there, John, Im-hotep, Winston, Mahatma, Bob, Sun and Thomas... so many masters of thought spiraling outward in infinite chains. And the greatest thing about them was that they had long abandoned tactics of deception. They were far beyond the simplicity of the present. The only way they got to where they were now was by using tactics that are not pos-sible unless freedom of testable information is available. Freedom of verifiable information was in fact the founda-tion of all the advanced complexities they were working with.

You could see it in their actions. They were all open and free to question each other's positions, and they did so repeatedly, ever faster. I was watching an accelerated ar-gument. An infinitely constructive argument... No ill will. None of the delay that occurs when aggressive idiots stop the debate to fight over the fact that one questioned the other or one offended the other.

26

"Be fruitful and multiply!" Damn, I remembered this short snippet from the bible well, as did most other people. But it was applied only to human beings. It did not describe how this was something that naturally occurred in many processes on earth. Not just human beings, and not just living things. It was everywhere, and only recently in the present had its non-living forms gotten described in enough detail to finally understand. They called them self-organizing processes. They called them chaotic dynamics. Amongst some other things... essentially these terms described anything in nature that multiplied itself exponentially by itself. Any process of growth that accelerated itself... Human beings were finding that this process was underneath every system of organization they had ever constructed. And initially, humans had ignorantly wanted it to be this way. Every institution in every society would grow ever faster, if it could find things to feed its growth. And organizations, even though they were not living things, would naturally pursue the paths that grew organizations faster. All systems of order perpetuated themselves off this feeding (*autocatalytic*) process. So what was the food? To quote a famous film from a little before the present, *"It's made out of people."*

How could structures of authority feed off of people? Wasn't it the people who set up those organizations? Didn't they do it for their benefit? They certainly didn't do it to destroy themselves. From the scope of hundreds or thousands of years ago, an idea of self-destruction through such a process must've seemed far off on the horizon if there at all. And initially, these organizations did give a lot of benefits to *some* of the people around. And admittedly, to a certain extent, all people around. But this point of thought should never be the end of inquiry. Again, things were not so simple.

Most of the feeding was merely on people's labor. Merely. Hah. People's time... That most precious element of life... But the collective of any country's organizations had human blood in its mouth. Especially the most powerful countries... War was their game. And so far in human history war had been one of the fastest ways to grow any country's bureaucracies. People tended to respond productively to threat and necessity. Necessity was the more valuable of the two. But threat was usually the necessity people thoughtlessly used to grow power. Necessity had much more complex incarnations than just the threat of survival. In fact most leaps in technology happened because of different necessities, other than threats. Threat was the initial crude layer of necessity, with an infinite amount of more fluid layers emerging out of it. Threat was the weakest, dumbest, and least successful impetus to discovery. But humans did not currently understand things to this depth. We did not have much time to learn.

I met with some of the most prominent leaders of fundamentalist Christianity. These days they had over a quarter of the total American population under their political control. I asked them all about how this made them feel. I asked them how it felt to receive that much of the gift of authority. All of them said very similar things, which I did not doubt would happen. They were all happy about it. They very much enjoyed the power my father's name had given them. They sought even more. They almost unanimously told me that 25% was not enough. They wanted 100%. Even when I reminded them that having everyone under your authority is not practically feasible, that with sixty percent they would effectively have total control. They did not seem to understand the impossibility of having a totally brainwashed army of followers. So they were still very far from realizing that having 'followers' at all was spiritually empty. When I asked them about this, that blank stare happened to them. Too much momentum had built up in their minds already, and too much power had given them inflated views of themselves and those most closely connected to them. They were not ready to give up that authority. They knew that the next terrorist attack that happened in the United States... would bring them another 25%.

They did not understand, mostly because they were unwilling to understand. A complex bureaucratic force largely the result of emergent properties of entropy itself was not something they had considered. Their rejection of evolution was evidence of that. I say that because evolution is also an emergent property of entropy itself, perhaps that distinction needn't even be drawn. Evolution is these days often thought to be entropy, acting on earth as it is in heaven. That's not really that accurate, but it sounds good.

Many people were trying to alert their fellow countrymen to the dangers of this authoritarian influence of Christian fundamentalists. But when it came to the fundamentalists themselves, (usually the most bigoted of the population), they saw any criticism of them as the only example of bigotry that they ever recognized. Self-centered was the name of the game these days. Even though that behavioral condition had only arisen due to massive societal forces. At least, those societal forces outweighed any personal will on the part of those that were self-centered. I know that position well. I've been the epitome of it before. I'm still getting over it.

As I said, the largest element of self-centeredness, strangely, was not within any person, but was in fact a property of the bureaucracy itself. The structure and momentum of these huge beasts perpetuated themselves endlessly. Really, the institutions just wanted to grow fast. As fast as they could. Ever faster... And since before this was known human beings unknowingly interrupted its growth, it did not care if they died in order to knock down that interruption. You think the cold war between the United States and the Soviet Union just happened by chance? It did not. The overall interconnected bureaucratic system on earth was attracted toward that position. Throughout the history of human beings creating bureaucratic institutions, those institutions were collectively moving toward the arrangement whereby the whole grew as quickly as it possibly could. The cold war served as a means of unprecedented growth. Bureaucracies are not alive. But their dynamics of growth have some of the properties of living things.

27

It was getting close to my birthday again. Or, what people thought was my birthday. Unfortunately for all of us, this birthday was going to be different. Those interests & people involved in escalating the Middle East conflict to an exponential and infinitely horrible scale needed their next move to be the framing of the conflict as a holy war. This was very easy to do. It had been done to more minor degrees many times before in history. All you have to do is attack your enemy on their favorite religious holiday. And of course, the largely ignorant teammates of Islamic fundamentalists and Western authoritarians (backed largely by Christian fundamentalists) were planning for an attack to occur on Christmas. That day people held so close to their rigid beliefs because they thought that day really was my birthday. Of course, as I inferred, it wasn't my birthday. But that didn't matter to them. The belief was all that was important to them. The meaning of that day had been created to make everyone's psychology respond as if a god had been born on that day. Religious holidays really were the perfect setup for disaster and disappointment.

Pat had foretold that in 2007 a serious terrorist attack would again happen in the United States. It would be a year similar to 2001. This was not his usual mad rambling. This prophecy had purpose behind it beyond that of the normal, whether Pat knew it or not. The people that had given Pat this impression had a particular goal in mind, one I have already discussed. To pre-write history, and to legitimate one those in power desired to be a leader. Whether Pat knew it or not, because of these people's intentions, all his years of guessing would mean he was due to finally be right with a silly prediction. This time Pat was going to be the miracle seer that god spoke through. Legitimacy would no longer be a problem for him. For once he will get respect from almost every American. And no one will suspect foul play.

News channels had been promoting the idea of a terrorist attack by Hezbollah. This was largely because of tensions with Iran, and the desire of the Bush administration (a Western authoritarian team) to have a good reason to attack Iran militarily. An attack on American soil by Hezbollah would be just the justification they needed. So would many other things, however. The administration seemed to be lining up as many potential pretexts as possible, with the knowledge that one of them would surely eventually pan out. And even beyond their desire to attack Iran, they were promoting Hezbollah as an adversary. Hezbollah & Israel had already recently succeeded with this *'promoting adversaries'* relationship. Authoritarian Western leaders wanted to grow their Western bureaucracies off of Hezbollah, while at the same time Hezbollah grew its organization's power off of them. So even if the Bush administration had already attacked Iran's nuclear facilities, or some limited strike of that nature, Hezbollah attacking inside the United States would still be valuable to them.

Al-Qaida was still around as an enemy for the West to build power off of, but Western bureaucracies wanted to expand their opportunities by promoting other adversaries into powerful worldwide organizations. Eventually the plan was for all the Islamic fundamentalist forces to meld together into a Middle East-wide alliance that would 'oppose' the Western alliance. Both supposedly opposing sides also needed their historic clash to be viewed mainly in religious terms. Just as Sunni & Shia Muslims had been coaxed into conflict with each other in the Middle East, Christians and Muslims were to be coaxed into conflict with each other on a worldwide scale (Muslim sects are eventually coaxed to reunite again to complete this). This was the higher level scope of what Satan had said they called *plan B*. This overall conflict was very complex. Each plan layer's divisions had other internal divisions that were being exploited. Bifurcation in alliance formation was the complexity theory specialty they were using to achieve these ends. Holy war was near the top of the hierarchy of conflicting divisions. It was one of the main goals of the endeavor. Holy war was the only way that very knowledgeable and largely secular Americans would support the increasing authoritarian structure of their lives in America. Suppression to a religion was the only way to guarantee that they would accept losing their freedom. Manipulating people's beliefs into supporting a new world war was also most achievable through manipulating people into a fundamentalist version of their religion. Who would not rally around Christianity after an attack on Christianity's most important day? If Americans did not realize that fundamentalists on both sides of this coming worldwide conflict were promoting each other as adversaries, America would lose democracy and become a totalitarian and largely theocratic empire.

Hezbollah or al-Qaida would use American authorities and be used by American authorities in this sense. I will not mention anything further because doing so may contribute to the causality of the event. Just know that each side in this fate-manufacturing clash of the West vs. Islam was counting on a Christmas attack to further rearrange and solidify alliances. Knowing and exposing this to the public is one of the only ways to stop it from happening. Even though it wasn't really my birthday, I was going to be very pissed if that day was used to help step up the conflict into a holy world war. The terrorist organizations would likely still try to do the attack. But if a significant proportion of the American population knew what the attack was intended to do, they would not let the attack have the psychological effect the leaders on both sides wanted. And so they would succeed in stopping both sides from accelerating the conflict.

This is all very complex, and it is not likely that any public of any country could be warned enough for such an event. But we must try. Or else the fundamentalists and authoritarians on both sides of the 'West vs. Islam' created conflict will win, and the future of the world will suffer miserably. Fate had the momentum of this occurring because of the momentum of the world's organizations growing at a more and more rapid pace. I remembered what Martin said. *"The great tragedy has an early head start."* We could make them grow faster on other pathways that avoided worldwide war. Any conflict can be averted when this is recognized and the bureaucratic growth is redirected. Holy war is what the authorities on both sides wanted. The public on both sides can reject this if they know their authorities are trying to trick them into it through this massive violence. All both publics have to do is not react violently to any attacks. Reactionary idiocy is what the authorities expect from their publics. They will continue to feed on this as long as the publics do not understand the trick. Terrorism must be treated as a matter of criminal justice and not war. Otherwise terrorism grows *and* your society turns more autocratic. This choice is not merely a strategic preference. This is the society's very survival. "Do not ever let authorities feed on you. You do not taste good." I told myself.

28

    Satan and I started doing interviews on television and radio. Of course I was the only one talking. I was the only one seen. It was quite monotonous to be on TV. Each different show you were on likely had mostly different viewers than the one you had done before. So you had to repeat almost the same set of statements every damn time. Or else people would not understand you well enough, according to what people here called marketing experts. Here are some of the things I had to keep saying in response to interviewers' questions.

    "I don't want you to think that I think I'm the Messiah or something like that. I don't care about that shit. That's just my insurance policy. I don't believe in any of that. I don't think I'm Jesus. I don't know what the hell there is after this place. And any description will just make this place that *we are in now* worse. I wasn't even in any of those strange places before... I just thought it all up to use it as a back-story for effect. I'm comfortable saying that I have no proof or significant idea about the totality of the universe let alone any supernatural (*whatever that means*) entity out there pulling strings. There's always more to learn. And there will always be things we haven't figured out yet. So I said, fuck it. With a perpetually unsolvable philosophical problem, I'm comfortable saying *I don't know*. When it comes to a description there is nothing. The description of such an infinite & ultimate concept must be blank. Nothing. Not that there is nothing, but you call the totality of it by no name. Not even the word "it". It is simply too large to be encompassed by any description. Any description offends the idea itself, lowering what is supposedly defined considerably below where words are sufficient in defining what they claim to define, so those words have no value or purpose (*or meaning*) at all in the first place.

Because of this, words that describe god at all actually produce a negative effect because they are words that are empirically *incorrect*. Because that much *is* testable... And so for a description there should be nothing.

No value, no meaning and no purpose (*a.k.a. a sufficiently incomplete description*) produce a negative value. And in the case of religion it is a very violent negative. This is not to say that religion should not exist. Just be *very careful* how literal your religion is with descriptions. However, this care should never be imposed from outside a religion. The people inside them need to understand the importance and high value of doing so themselves. As the hand had told me, just about all of the world's religions already have a form of this somewhere in their, 'rules & regulations' sections. They just don't usually abide by it. If pointed out honestly and directly, no religion will be able to deny they are violating these inherent rules of their faiths. And at the same time, no government would be able to implement a religion in the form of a government, especially even an atheist government, as had been mistakenly done before as well.

I'm just a guy that read a bunch of books through the years and thought about combining the thoughts I got from them in strangely interesting ways. Anyone can do that. To make a point about where we're at now. And where we might be in a hundred years if we're not intelligent enough in our decision making now. That's an important function of a thinking being. You have to be able to see where you're going. It may seem repetitive, but it's an infinitely productive & calculated repetition."

Quite controversial was the response (*usually along with a very strange look*) I got in return from interviewers, unless they had already read the book. With respect to one interviewer however, I had a slightly different idea about how to discuss the purpose of our PR campaign. I wondered if he'd play along.

"Bill, now you know what I'm going to say to the question you've got to ask me. So when you ask me I'm going to steer the conversation to silence, making it look obvious that I'm dodging your question or not able to answer it. I'm going to assume that you know I'm going to do that because you've read the book and you understand what I'm doing here. Because you respect fate, and nonlinear public relations techniques, you're going to play along. But I don't even have to say that on the air, because you've already read it. And other people can read it, if they want to know too. Bill, you are trying to help create world war three, the end of the world. You know that it is not really the end of the world, but it is still an unprecedented devastation to humanity through war and all that emerges from conditions of war worldwide. You should stop trying to do this. I smile at you on the air when I think this sentence. We will just stare at each other for this part of the interview while we think this paragraph, knowing exactly what the other is thinking, and some in the audience will know too. This is all in thought. You, me, and your audience... in thought together."

Then I started talking. To buffer the extreme oddity that was silence, which is so rare on TV. "You know what I saw in an American magazine the other day? A watch advertisement with an idealized picture of Napoleon Bonaparte on it... The ad said he owned a timepiece from the same company back in his day. The company was using a historical dictator to sell watches to Americans. As if Napoleon deserves respect and admiration. A tyrant... being the spokesman for a product that's for sale in the United States! An expensive ad for an expensive watch that wouldn't be in the magazine if it hadn't been market tested first. Some Americans were walking around showing their new watch off to their friends flaunting the fact that Napoleon owned the same kind. As if they themselves felt the phony prestige of a dictator by wearing it. American culture was being changed. Democracy was fading at an accelerated pace. And you Bill, much more than this watch ad, have helped to make that happen. How does that make you feel?" For this question he had no answer. For his answer we again stared in silent thought. The asymmetrical reflection of what had just previously happened.

After I had done most of these interviews… as Satan and I were hanging out in another hotel room amidst our little predestined public relations campaign, I thought about the possibility of a potentially critical mistake. I had been exposing the plan to cause the end of the world. Was there the possibility that I might help to cause their end of the world plan to work better through my obsession of stopping it? Even if I didn't directly cause any part of it, could I cause those involved to speed up the implementation of their plan so as to lock it in before the world public's knowledge could take effect and prevent it? *"No."* He seemed so sure. I asked him why. *"Because the causal forces behind the plan, are already more than sufficient to cause the plan without our involvement. Therefore any involvement by you or anyone else moving nonviolently against the overall plan (be careful – many subsections of the plan are designed to trick opposition into making it worse) cannot add to something that would already be happening because of the people already implementing it on both sides. So it would be very hard for **you** to make it worse. There are plenty of actors in this game that are already trying to do that."* Coming from him I still wasn't sure. He was known as the ultimate deceiver. *"I'm a fake! Remember?! And in this drama, I'm here to help. We have rewritten the rules."*

29

The age of nations was coming to a close, and hardly anyone living in a nation realized it. There had been newer more fluid institutional layers emerging from older, bigger, slower ones. And yet the prominent theory of the day that was being latched onto was that an even bigger, slower, and older institutional layer was forming (there was only enough space on earth for a couple of these of course). That layer was the civilization. Why would we return to an old monolith of this sort? Probably because of the desire for total world control and the perception that only something as big as a civilization could achieve such lofty ends.

Satan and I had been very busy in New York. We had been visiting with a great many media outlets, government officials, and what are called 'ordinary people' here. The term ordinary seems nonsensical to us, because most often times their lives are much more interesting than the lives of the powerful. They are so less obedient than the powerful. We had one more stop before we headed back to Washington D.C. We had a meeting, I mean, a speaking engagement, before the Council on Foreign Relations. This organization had quite the reputation in the present. Apparently, some people thought they were behind some conspiracy for world government, and others thought they were just a group that had smart people in it with specialties on foreign policy and so their views were given more weight. Most people did not even know the organization existed, but that could only be blamed on ignorance because no one was hiding the organization. Maybe they hid some of the stuff they talked about or dealt with. That wasn't going to be the case with today's meeting however. Today Satan was golden. He was more excited about this meeting than any of the others we had done, and I was beginning to wonder why. Maybe he knew something I didn't.

"Of course I do." He said. *"You should just assume that is always the case, hah."* Inspiring confidence was one of his strong points. Deflating confidence had been one of mine. I wasn't sure what he had planned, and since he wouldn't tell me, I couldn't prepare for the meeting. So I just figured I'd wing it. *"Don't worry about it. Worrying will only fuck you up."* As we walked down East 68th Street, we got a lot of looks from everyone. We stood out. It was just myself in somewhat tattered clothes, walking down the street. But it seemed like people could tell there were other minds amidst my presence. The Council had to take special security precautions given the notoriety of the visit. I had said publicly already that I thought myself to be just a man, albeit one who thinks a lot. Nothing supernatural about me... But the 'man' I was working with was known to be one of the most arrogant and manipulative beings in the history of the universe. No one could see Satan. As far as anyone was concerned he was a figment of my imagination, which I admitted was probably the case, although I referred to him and what he was doing on occasion.

We had the full attention of some of the world's most powerful people. Many others had come on this day given the circumstances of our visit. They wanted to hear what would be said. There were so many interests involved. Satan looked around and told me, *"These people think they're the most clever in the world. And they still haven't gotten to the point of realizing there are infinite levels to clever, and relative to many things, living things even on earth, these people are so simple it's a joke."* I was called to the podium to deliver my speech. But I had written no speech. I think they intended for me to talk about all of the things we had been discussing in our PR campaign. But I did not have any reference in which to discuss. Satan said calmly in response to my anxiousness, *"It's time for some of my favorite things."*

The room was ominously quiet. When I got before the podium, Satan propelled into action. Despite his reputation, he was not into wasting time. I heard a voice cry out from the audience, "*I offer you the kingdom of Saudi Arabia! It is yours to rule!*" The crowd was instantly confused, because yelling out during events was frowned upon. It was not usually done, especially saying such crazy things as what had been yelled out. Everyone there wondered who had screamed such a ridiculous comment. At that moment I knew that Satan had possessed someone in the crowd and made them yell out the comment. And at that moment, I knew his plan. I responded to the offer. "The kingdom of Saudi Arabia probably seems very valuable to all of you, but it is really devoid of value, (even though it currently holds some value), because it is an autocratic system. It prevents value from developing. Therefore any value it has is going to be lost probably sooner than later. I do not want such a failure as a possession. The millions of people living in Saudi Arabia deserve much better than their present circumstance. Thanks though." Another person in the crowd then yelled out "*What about the nation of Germany? Will you accept our gracious gift of Germany?*" Satan was being very funny. But he had a profound point in doing this. "No. I do not want Germany. Although these days it has more value because it is much more free than it has previously been. But to give any small group of people control over it, let alone one person, would destroy any value it has." "*What about the United States?*" Someone else in the crowd cried. "*Will you join our Western alliance by taking the presidency there?*" "No. Any presidency is still too dynamically close to a king or a dictator. Democracies need to get past a singular leader in all respects. And your planned Western alliance is merely an attempt to concentrate the power of Western democracies into fewer hands. Such a plan is an intentional disaster. Such a plan will only destroy value, destroy profit, and destroy freedom. I'm astonished that Western minds thought of it, let alone allowed it to persist. Why people still desire autocratic systems over increasingly democratic systems, is a mystery to almost all scientists." The crowd gasped.

Satan continued this quite hilarious process of possessing people in the crowd and going through every form of government and offering me every form of authority in it. Each time I rejected it with very good reason. It inhibited profit. Authority prevented value from being added. It prevented growth. Then someone offered up, *"I give you control of the Vatican, the descendent of your very church. Rule as the Pope from now on!"* "No way." I said immediately. "I don't want that broken thing. That church betrayed most of the things I ever said in my message my first time around. And nobody noticed. Even those churches that later separated from it. They behaved quite similarly. No church should want power. And I want no power over any church." The crowd again gasped with what must have been enlightenment.

Satan was not done yet, he had one more offering to make before me. One of the most powerful people in the ranks of the CFR was possessed, and spouted off uncontrollably, *"Would you like to rule the world? I can give it to you!"* While Satan was possessing these people and making them say these things, he had to use their own thoughts. They all thought these systems of control were valuable, and they all thought that a ruler of the world was possible, even beneficial. They really were some of the most simple minds on the whole of the earth. They were the minds that accepted the most discipline and obedience throughout their entire lives. These things they held as more precious than anything. They had succeeded in suppressing nearly every inclination of freedom of thought in their own lives for their entire lives. And that is why they had ascended through all hierarchies to the very top levels. I had one thing to say to minds as simple as this. "No one can rule the world! EVER. By trying to rule it, you will only destroy life in the world. No one will ever achieve a centralized power over all people on earth. Stop trying. You are inhibiting your own power. I would have no part in such a suicidally stupid idea. You all are too simple to even think it possible. You must reject such power fantasies. They prevent you from achieving more power, although you do not yet see it that way. You will soon. All systems of control prevent you from achieving more power. This may sound nonsensical to you. But I assure you it makes perfect sense. It is merely nonlinear. It is more complex than your mind has yet experienced. Allow your mind to experience it, and all value and power will accelerate."

Satan and I confidently but humbly walked out of the building after this, as the crowd nervously pondered what usually their fear of not being obedient (and their fears of each other) would prevent them from thinking. People had once described me as the king of kings. But I didn't want to be king of anything. The sky outside the building in New York shined with a new flavor. We had done well. Now they knew. Now we needed to continue telling others. We were living in a consolidation phase of existence. And it had gone way too far in that direction already. Reversing was necessary.

30

"*I'm not promoting world war three!*" Newt insisted. I reminded Newt that he could not lie to me. That I know what he's done, and I know what he's thought. I told him he has consistently promoted the idea to Americans that we're already in world war three. I know, as Newt knows, the effect this will have psychologically on the population. I know that he's saying world war three every other day on TV to repeat the framework within which he desires the American public's mind to be. "*I want to win this war! I want America to defeat the Islamists. I'm trying to defeat them.*" He insisted. I informed him of his own thoughts, that he was trying to first build an enemy of militant Islam from relative obscurity into a worldwide power, and *then* defeat that power, taking long enough for all the government bureaucracy building, changing world alliances and borders, and adequate levels of industrial profit to have been achieved. To accomplish the transformation program within the US military and intelligence bureaucracies and US society toward an increasingly authoritarian structure... He interrupted me again. "*America has long term strategic interests that need to be met! This is the way it has always worked. Why should we give up our position of authority in the world when some country that hates us would take our place?*" The simplicity of his thoughts was hilarious to me. Not uncommon here of course.

Damn. I had hoped to draw him into this sort of honesty on the air. "Power is not a zero sum game." I told him. I would think someone of his prominence would recognize this already. "Authority inhibits the growth of power in the age of accelerated technological growth." I wondered if this statement would confuse him or he would realize the increasing freedom that was destined to come with the natural exponential growth of technology. I assumed he would've already realized that authoritarianism was going to end as a tactic of bureaucrats and politicians. Abandoned for better techniques. And although corporations are more dynamic organizations than whole governments, they still operate in a totalitarian model of authority. Just in case he didn't realize all of this already I hit him with one of the arguments that changed their minds. "Don't you realize the position you're in? You're on the verge of making the case that national governments need to be abandoned as organizations. You and your allies in this mess are proving this point whether you know it or not, and I'm sure some of you do. You're effectively destroying the American government. You're going to bankrupt the country on purpose. Wouldn't be the first time people did that to a country. This time it would be for an additionally important reason. It could destroy most of the government bureaucracies, freeing all corporations from any and all regulation. As I said, some of you know this is happening, and you gladly await the post-national corporate rule of as much of earth as you can get. And it's not entirely a bad plan... if what you're going for is a large deviation from a stable equilibrium, which Joseph proved in the early twentieth century, is the main source of profit. But the way you're implementing the plan is unnecessarily violent. And it remains a bad plan as long as the corporate bureaucratic structures are anywhere near as totalitarian in nature as the governments they replaced. Which they are... sometimes worse even... They must be so much more fluid than that... they must progressively lessen authority and lessen control of everyone indefinitely. They must reject becoming an empire and reject the tendency toward increasing the size & control of any company (*or government*) past a certain point. The real violent *force* behind totalitarian structures must be dealt with. This includes any agency or bureaucracy (*or company*) that is security, defense, or war related. Their authority must lessen with time, or business loses.

136

Society loses. As has happened too many times before, an opposing authoritarian response will naturally and surely take over any remotely autocratic system, no matter if it is corporate or government in name. No matter how powerful it is. This is the nature of nature. To prevent this, industries that produce violence must end. Just as human slavery, war must end as a business." So many things needed to be said. I wondered if he was getting it all.

"Newt, I understand they intend for you to be president or vice president. And if not, you will be put in the administration of the president. You are what they call a *'primary tier in the contingency map'*. With the job of continuing the transfer of American power into fewer and fewer hands under the current authoritarian momentum." He came back with the usual ignoring of that which he wished people not to know. *"That's not what's happening. Our agencies need to communicate better. They need to be more connected, with someone in charge of all of them so that they can work better."* I laughed. "You know full well that combining all the bureaucracies under a direct and non-competing singular authority figure lessens freedom substantially, which lessens communication as well." *"You have to trade some freedom for security, and most Americans understand this reality."* He responded. I laughed again. "No you don't. And the only reason some Americans believe that to be the case is because they do not know their country's history and they are just parroting what authoritarians like you say on TV back when prompted. Freedom should never be traded for security. If freedom is at any time traded for security, America will lose both freedom and security. Benjamin told me this directly. He told me to tell you to stop what you're doing."

I knew that Newt knew that many Americans, even some in government, knew that trading freedom for security was a false choice. But they did not take the next critical step of realizing that those that promote the idea of trading freedom largely know that it will lessen security and hence give their political party more concentrated power. These certain politicians and officials are effectively betraying the American system of representative government in favor of a militaristic authoritarian state. Benjamin told me that the Bill of Rights to the Constitution was designed to prevent this, as it is a list of anti-totalitarian-government protective mechanisms that must be extended in number, not eroded away. And leaders that *did* know that American authoritarians are using a false choice to trick the public into giving up their freedom... did nothing to stop the authoritarians. They just sat back quietly as America was taken over from within. And I told Newt all of this. He was nervously avoiding conversation at this point, because any response could validate any certain part of what I had said. And it occurred to me at this point that even he was afraid of authority. Even though he was one of the top members of that authority. He was very afraid. His thoughts were fast and disjointed now, flashing the faces and names of some of the people he feared could learn about this conversation. Even though he had not betrayed them in it. His mere participance in it could put him in jeopardy, or so his paranoid thoughts thought. He attempted to leave. I reminded him of the role I was playing, and that he was safe talking to me.

"Don't be so sure. We all watch each other to prevent leaks." I reminded him that I had no evidence, nor did I need any evidence, to substantiate any impropriety on their part. I, and others were figuring out scientifically what was happening to all the world's bureaucracies, proposing hypotheses, and allowing the public to test each hypothesis. Brainstorming over brainwashing. I only helped let some ideas out to be tested. He was still very anxious. "Calm down Newt. Didn't you hear? You no longer need to be afraid of authority. Scientifically tested information is now the only legitimate authority. And since this is now known, any other authority is an irrational joke." This calmed him

momentarily as he pondered such repercussions. I continued, "Any authority that denies this, from this day forward, denies itself profit and power. And no intelligent authority would deny itself these things." I could see thought paths shift in his head. I could see learning taking place. I could see in him, representing a microcosm of everyone, greed and dominance redirecting their paths to achieve greater rewards.

This coming worldwide conflict was still not even necessarily coming. It was still under construction at this point. It could be stopped. And although some of the world's most powerful people were trying to make it happen, what they didn't know was that their plan was going to be stopped. They had calculated the whole endeavor spuriously. They neglected important data proving that the twenty-first century would be run by no country. Not even the United States of America. All countries that attempted such dominance would fail. And that failure would significantly weaken any country that tried. Any attempt at dominance by any country would also weaken the world. Even though I'm using the term right now, world war three was not going to happen. It should not happen. Everyone should do everything they can to remove representatives of power from influential positions if they in any way advocate fighting in such a disaster. Only those who comfortably think of themselves as mass murderers would support such a plan. World war three could be prevented by rational legal actions against authoritarians and terrorists in any countries involved in such a bureaucracy-building scheme.

And even though these guys had been using complexity theory, they had been using the knowledge in a crude and self-destructive manner. The fate of organizations such as Enron should have made that clear to everyone by now. They should know that they were directing the US government toward the same type of cataclysmic failure. I asked him if they were aware of that… were they just flat out intentionally destroying the US government from within, with intentions of immense profit amidst near total economic failure of government and the subsequent temporary failure of US markets? They would have inside knowledge. They would know what was going to happen. Because they were making it happen. And their money would be moved accordingly to the greatest possible benefit. At the cost of all other investors.

"So many big companies would be very upset with you if they knew this was going on," I reminded him. "And you can't possibly cut them all in."

31

The Caliphate was being constructed. It was bin Laden's dream. And he must've known how to get his enemies to help him build it. He knew what they wanted. He had used their military interventions in the Middle East as one of his main purposes for his organization to recruit supporters and operatives. Why would he also not use their continued military interventions in the Middle East to help him build the seemingly impossible Islamic Caliphate (effectively an empire) that encompassed the entire Middle East and beyond? And why would his enemies not let him? They would be using him as well in the process. They needed some grand opposition as the purpose of expanding their bureaucracies into an empire too. What better than a unified fundamentalist Middle Eastern enemy? *"Remember what you told me, it is important that you assert that this is not conspiracy. It's good complex military strategy. And it is a strategy feeding on an unbridled bureaucratic expansion force that no man controls. Bin Laden and Western authorities are very familiar with these types of forces and strategies."* "Agreed, thank you... thou art smarter than I." I told Satan.

Since bin Laden was not around anymore... and his organization would not like to talk to someone that represented Christianity, even though I was trying to undo the organized authorities of Christianity, I went to talk to some more of the Western authorities involved in this tango. Maybe they would see the stupidity of their actions. Although I was quite practical these days, I did not expect them to budge at all. I had only gotten Newt to think about it, nothing more... I expected as well that the rest would not give a damn what one random person thought. Even when that one person had just told everyone about how they could prove the authority's stupidity with experiments... But I still had to try. Since Dick was pretty much quarterbacking this end-game, I went to him next. I was surprised that he was so willing to see me. I knew then that he must've read my work. My introductory and closing remarks to this master of history, while corny, were quick and to the point, which I was told would be necessary.

"Dick, I know what you're trying to do. And I know that you'll probably succeed in getting it started. You've pretty much already played the hands that will get it started. But you will not succeed in continuing it. You're learning how messing with fate, for the purposes of violence, can come back to you in the most mysterious of ways." He laughed. I was immediately left with the impression that he thought this all to be a ridiculous publicity stunt. All I had to do was keep talking. "It's time for you to reveal it to them, Dick. It's time for you to tell them that the Iraq war was messed up on purpose. The military plan was from the beginning to destabilize the entire region starting with Iraq. You guys thought you were so clever. You tried to setup everything this time. You intended for an anti-war backlash in the US to politically force a pullout from Iraq. You're relying on that happening. Then you'll attempt to blame the destabilization of Iraq on what you'll call the Democratic 'retreat' (even though *your team destabilized Iraq on purpose*, Dick), causing a cultural backlash that changes the Democratic party to a more militarist & authoritarian party like the Republicans had been changed to many years ago. It is brilliant chess, but you forgot about many things."

He was no longer laughing. I must've said some things that I did not also write. He sat up in his chair, and tried to think of a way to cut me in, or cut me out. "Don't bother." I said. "I have already arranged everything for you. You knew this day would come." Although, I knew, he did not. He was probably perplexed in interesting ways, even though he knew most of what I was going to say before I said it. Because he had already read it... "It's time for you to tell everyone, Dick. And it's also time, to really change your tactics. Your secret plan will not work. I know that you do not know this. And I surely know that you will not believe my words asserting this. You should've studied nonlinear dynamics more before trying so arrogantly to implement them on a world-wide scale." Then I left his office, knowing full well whom he would have to call... and what they would have to talk about.

They understood that I had a value to them. So again, even though I was in opposition to their plans, they would use me, and I would use them. I had goals of dissipating authority. They had goals of creating the end of the world scenario from the bible. I would play a small part in their necessary 'savior returns to earth' role. And they would end up changing their societies to stop the world-wide conflict that all sides had intentionally started. They knew that what I had told them was inevitable. And so now I would help them unmake their mess. They would not be able to continue the business of war anymore. Capitalism had more to gain elsewhere. And we had showed them these places. Places where profit far exceeded that of defense companies' wildest dreams. Places where government bureaucracies would no longer inhibit any capitalist economic growth, as all government agencies (*especially the ones related to security*) would increasingly go the way of the dinosaur. And any combination of government and company would be abandoned as an idea. Just as any combination of religion and government had been abandoned (*in some societies*) hundreds of years ago. And so the age of fascism would really be over. They had finally seen how abandoning certain industries (*the industries in any way tied to war or government, unless they untied them from war or government*) was going to be necessary for a new phase of capitalist freedom. And they wanted that money so badly. "*More money than god.*" Adam had told me.

143

32

"Nasrallah!" I yelled before crowds as we traveled the country. "Ahmadinejad! Bin Laden! You are betraying your people in order to gain power for yourselves!" "Bush!" I continued to yell. "Cheney! Perle! You are betraying your people in order to gain power for yourselves!" I knew none of them cared. They all thought they were doing the '*right*' thing. All sides thought they were gaining power for their people as well, not only for themselves and their societies' ruling parties. For their country, they thought. I mean, they said publicly. I guess they did not really think it.

Nonlinear dynamics was being twisted into death when it showed such promise in areas other than war. Organizations have been using complex schemes involving intentional failures. The wider goal was sometimes success, but also sometimes failure. Enron is an example where the overall plan was actually failure. Although most involved in these complex networks of deception usually think the overriding plan is for success, it can go either way. And you never really know who's aiming for what when deception gets that complex. Probably at least more than one person involved in any such deception is preparing for both, to protect themselves and to capitalize off of either eventuality.

Complex organizational schemes involving intentional failure were seeping into the wider culture as well. They were not just reserved for the militaries of societies. And this overexposure threatened their secrecy. Pop-culture had run amuck with publicity scam after publicity scam milking similar techniques. In addition every so-called 'reality show' on American TV exemplified it to millions of people daily. Turns out, the self-organization property that grew both publicity and bureaucracy was using the same physical force. Manufacturing conflict (*intentional instability*) was a very visible part of the culture. It could not be kept secret. It was a newly revealed deception principle in capitalism itself. Every business would try to use the techniques. The techniques would become old and easily recognizable, like that of the one-less-digit or one-less-number mark of the beast deception. This was to be, in effect, a new mark of the beast. That creating conflict grew businesses.

I did not fight this development. I redirected this development away from the self-destructive and toward the even greater growth. Business would need to perpetually increase competition, effectively increasing conflict between organizations. But this conflict would be competitive in nature. Not violent. Anytime competitive conflict got caught in an accelerated trajectory toward becoming violent, practical measures would be taken to prevent it from undoing its own interest.

Prophecy was not only being used on the Western side. The desired Islamic fundamentalist alliance side as well had planned for saviors and prophets to come. The establishment of the new Caliphate was such an attempt to bring about ancient prophecy. No matter what side people were on in this plan, they were trying to grab hold and direct time... fate itself. On the Western side certain people were going to Jerusalem trying to get the Temple rebuilt to help fulfill that part of prophecy. We had even seen a plan by some to actually construct a realistic looking battle of Armageddon to fool the world. Satan and I were trying to disrupt any side's fulfillment of such psychotic plans. They were all feeding into each other's fundamentalist psychosis. Both sides expected to gain from unprecedented worldwide destruction. They needed to be dealt with. Each side's leaders were failing a simple test of rationality. I expect smart people to placate them.

But smart people had yet to do this. The US had even set the stage for the most serious escalation in terrorist violence. The nuclear attack... *"These sick bastards on both sides want it to happen."* Satan interjected. "I know." I told him. But al-Qaida, despite getting a supposed 'official religious legitimacy' (*from a small group of psychos that did not really represent the religion of Islam – they represented an institutional bureaucracy that was using a religion*) to use such a weapon... didn't yet have dynamical legitimacy. In the sense of, in tit-for-tat, you can't have tat without tit first. Nuclear weapons were going to be used by the Western side initially. But they were going to be used in a new, 'smaller' sense. This new technology developed that supposedly limited the effects of nuclear weaponry, called bunker busters on TV. How they got people to believe that small nuclear weapons were ok to use was evidence of their society's increasingly totalitarian structure. So like all things that come into being, this event sequence would start out small. Iran was the likely target. This, even though supposedly small, *physically* legitimizes the use of nuclear weapons once again in war & terrorism.

This circumstance itself of course is a horrible mistake that as I said is more evidence of critical totalitarian-level influence in Western governments because many layers of bureaucracy *should* have prevented such developments. If any sense of checks, balances and democracy remained within their military structures... it would have never come close to happening.

It was obvious that the majority of the current Islamic world was totalitarian. That was largely a result of colonialism and imperialism, not Islam. And the West was going to mix with them violently. As previously hypothesized, this assured that both sides would mix by taking on their autocratic traits rather than both sides becoming more of a democracy. It also assured that the West would make Islamic countries more totalitarian than they already were.

Both sides would increasingly autocratize each other until they both died. That was what mixing violently would produce. Mixing peacefully, cooperatively, with respect for the obviously necessary differentiation of cultures, would produce increasingly more democratic societies on both sides. This is what the mixing would have to be changed to. And while it seems a long shot to redirect both sides away from the current method being employed... after what *I am* says is demonstrated via experiment it will be increasingly easy to convince idiots that they're clubbing themselves in the head.

Satan changed the subject, *"Complexity expands in every direction. That includes size as well. What people hadn't realized yet though is that the size of the earth itself inherently has a cap on organizational size and the concentrated control of its power. Civilizations, as an institutional layer, were going to be very short lived indeed. Some historians even doubt whether they ever existed or they would be more aptly described as just far reaching empires, which now everyone should know have their own increasingly short shelf-life."*

Yes... having a clash of civilizations could only do 1 thing... destroy societies. The most complex deceptions were never as complex as the simplest cooperation, although this was not usually thought about in this way. This was particularly noticeable when the complex deceptions involved phony cooperation. I had been given an internal assessment said to be from inside the highest level of the American military structure. Satan had somehow stolen it. *"You know how easy it is to fool all those idiots in bureaucracies!"* "Yes, I know... especially the people at the highest levels of bureaucracy." It said many things that we had already been saying publicly. *"It's part of plan B."* He said. It was dated *May 16th, 1999*. We made sure that this official version of what we were revealing got to every damn media outlet in the world. It began quite simply:

- **Prophecy is written in order** *to be made into reality* **later in time by religious zealots. It is** obviously **not some mystical act of god. It will be made to look that way by the violent zealots we create & recruit. The utmost care must be taken when implementing each operational layer of this for maximum effect. Current leaders of all countries based on the religions of Christianity, Judaism & Islam are to be intentionally coaxed into attempting to fulfill end time prophecies for the collection of our externally outlined political & economic goals. The whole plan's semi-end state is to be largely based on Huntington's "Clash of Civilizations" paper & book.**

Satan was so pissed. But I guess he was always sort of pissed. *"They are trying to take the chance out of history. Do they realize how stupid that is? No. They pursue it in genetics. They pursue it in their political and economic structures. Changing an open system into a closed system by removing any chance events is suicide for everything in nature. They think they're smarter than nature already. They can't even mimic the simplest movements of smoke, water, or fire in their own motion, let alone create their own more complex motions (that require the allowance of even more real statistical chance) and they think they're smarter than these things? Natural selection did not keep randomness in its program because it is stupid. Humans have so much to learn. They are so ignorant, that they think they can actually direct the future itself!"* I read on:

- **Authoritarian elements within different opposing societies should move toward the same goal of concentrating & extending the power of both those authoritarian sides by engaging in limited conflicts.**

  - ○ **Terrorist organizations add a new level of complexity to this authoritarian relationship,**

although the same effect remains and is to be exploited.

- **al-Qaida can exist & grow only if they have an authoritarian government that will "fight" them so they can feed off of this authoritarian relationship. We must exploit this as well as possible. Of course because of this we do not attempt to dismantle their senior leadership. Although because of their asymmetrical and decentralized organizational structure our foot-dragging is only a temporary concern.**

- **Hezbollah, a terrorist organization known to be connected to the government of Iran, should also be used in this mutually beneficial authoritarian relationship with the United States to enhance these ends with regards to our Iranian program.**

It is highly probable that al-Qaida will *someday* attack again inside the United States. It is also highly probable that Hezbollah will *someday* attack for the first time inside the United States. It is in the interest of both sides (*US authoritarians & any terrorist orgs.*) that this happens. This interest is yet to be checked. It needs to be, because it is highly probable that, when any terrorist attacks happen, authoritarians within the US government will use these attacks to consolidate the power of all military & intelligence bureaucracies (*and to grow their own power over these agencies*), removing more and more freedom every time an attack occurs... making **both** the terrorist organizations and their opposing authoritarian counterparts **win** by turning the United States into a *god damned* autocratic empire.

Although it seemed to be, this document Satan re-covered wasn't enough. Many real people inside govern-ments & companies would have to give any similar docu-ments to every media outlet in the world. And many scien-tists would have to experiment with all these hypotheses and publicly publish the results. Because if these types of government secrets could not be exposed, or if these events were not so much directed secretly as they were the result of a natural nonlinear organizing process (*either way*), the science would be the key to ending terrorism *and* 'the war on terrorism'. Only then could it all be stopped. Satan ran-domly yelled out again, this time on a tangent with a strange if any relevance. *"You can't get into serious space travel (technologically speaking) without playing nice. Anyone else that may or may not be out there knows this… people are still like an ignorant and therefore wild animal to them. When people want to seriously accelerate their technology they'll give up and abandon war as a business."* Give up *and* abandon. That's redundant. He didn't seem to think he was mistaken in his communication of these words. *"I wasn't."* Still, it didn't matter. As he probably knew, we had already done what we came to do. We had succeeded. *"If the two best neglect the rest, the house of cards will fall…"* He meant the most powerful… the de-fense & energy industries. *"Capitalism should not want to destroy itself, but it just couldn't help it…   until now."*

150

33

"*What about poverty? Wasn't that supposed to be handled?*" Many people asked me this as I traveled. "When authority is dissipated, i.e. when wealth and power are dissipated, wealth and power will move at an accelerated pace toward more and more numbers of people. The rich will learn that they get richer faster by spreading the wealth. Especially when they *invest* in the very poorest. The powerful will learn that they get more power faster when they divide and spread all forms of power, especially to the least powerful. Both rich & powerful people currently think the opposite of this, but demonstrating the success of dissipation of wealth and power through experiments will guarantee that poverty is increasingly solved, along with so many other things." Satan jumped in laughing, "*They currently think dissipation means: To attenuate to or almost to the point of disappearing. To vanish by dispersion... Hah, what simplicity! In nonlinear dynamics dissipation is the key to accelerating growth! It does not disappear, it magnifies itself by dividing as it grows in scale!*" "Changing these socio-economic dynamics will change many aspects of every society that have gone unsolved since our beginning."

"*And what about all those descriptions of the time scale beyond the unfolding present? Now that we know how it works, won't that interfere with time here?*" People would also ask me. That answer was simple. "There's no need to worry about that. Because we succeeded in our mission, things post-life went back to the way they normally are. The way we don't know about. The way no one can know about." Consciousness will eventually know where it is going after this, I thought. But not for a long time... We have so much to learn yet. Be patient. If we're not patient it will postpone that eventuality much further.

Then I heard a voice echo through my head. "*Everyone's objective is convincing people of something. Why? Why have to convince anyone of anything? It is a situation derivative of communication itself. Why say anything if not to transmit some piece of information? The validity of that information matters. No one wants to absorb and use incorrect information. And yet to differing degrees, that is all anyone's ever done. Using and communicating increasingly provable information is our trajectory. That's where we're going. But we begin with such crude models of thinking. And we get attached to those early descriptions of reality. So much so that we're willing to die rather than give them up. So much so that deception runs rampant. That's not smart. At our human society starting line, we are without almost any empiricism. Even today, in the most highly technologically advanced society in the history of the world, the majority of the population does not even know what the word empiricism means.*"

Utopian systems always commit the dynamical fallacy of certainty and completeness. There is no certainty in the universe. Nothing in the universe is complete. No system of governance can ever be established as a complete and successful model. In fact any that would attempt to state such a claim or initiate that model in a society would in fact be attempting to initiate a totalitarian structure. As part of its definition a totalitarian society is an attempt at an absolutely ordered structure that never needs to change because it thinks and acts as if its current structure is perfect.

"*Perfect it is not. There is a larger structure to life, and we figure out what it is trying different things. The pattern makes sense. You can see how it fits. It's written well. It is structurally sound. Do not assume that the pattern is linear. While there are simple parts to patterns in nature, the vast majority of the pattern is nonlinear. If the structures we build are too simple, they break that part of the larger structure. We make boxes. We make circles. Almost everything we design is based on a square. This is way too simple. We were too dumb, understandably so, in the beginning. Don't continue to be that dumb. We must never assume that the current degree of complexity in the structures we design, are the best, complete, or correct. The larger structure is accelerating its complexity constantly. We must do this too. Be prepared to abandon old ideas. There is a larger structure to life, and we figure out what it is trying different things. Then we change those things by trying new things. Continue forever."*

Forever into the future... war, like slavery, had been abandoned as a viable business option. It was about damn time. Just like the slave holding companies of America's past, those companies that made military equipment, weapons, etc. had diversified into other markets and industries. Not because they were forced to by a government, but because they saw how the profit was exponentially greater to do so. Economics had succeeded in becoming a little bit closer to being a rigorous science like that of physics or chemistry. While all conflict on earth had not been totally solved, the main source of exponentially increasing that conflict had been dealt with. For now...

Now it actually looked like the future. When the number of parts in a system, grow to a certain quantity, the chaotic dynamics can emerge. 'Chaotic' in the mathematical sense, not any bad or evil sense. It merely means complex patterns, not directed by any one part of the whole, can emerge from conditions. Every part of the structure is free to pursue its own path. And all together, this freedom produces the complex pattern. We have been fruitful and we have multiplied. Redundancy and inefficiency have profound importance. We are now almost 7 billion in number. Human beings have finally achieved the necessary quantity. Now we can really begin our history.

"History looked back on from 2100 (or any point) could have been more or less violent. The clash of civiliza-

tions did not need to happen. World war three did not need to happen. So neither did. The people on all sides that had been trying to make it happen were convinced otherwise. It is almost always still possible to reverse a process (redirected out of danger really, no need to violate the 2nd law) on your own scale. The possibility is even more so if it's a process that people have any control over. Which is always the case as long as they recognize this. That's how it's built. That's just one of the properties every scale has. Any conflict can be prevented or resolved, i.e. fluidly reengineered once enough people know enough details about its inner workings. If increasingly more people can understand what's going on...they can change what's going on. This is a property of the free-fate/entropy/evolution/increasingly accelerated complex space-time expansion, whatever you wanna call it. Our whole time is an actual physical structure on a higher scale. It's already built, and yet this "built" constantly rebuilds differently. Change is this universe's most fundamental property. It makes us do it. Nicely at first."

about the author: